COCKED DICE
THE COMPLETE CASES OF
DAFFY DILL, VOLUME 1

OTHER BOOKS IN THE ARGOSY LIBRARY:

THE PHANTOM IN THE RAINBOW
SLATER LAMASTER

THREADS OF EVIDENCE: THE COMPLETE CASES OF RIORDAN, VOLUME 1
VICTOR MAXWELL

MASTERS OF DARKNESS
MURRAY LEINSTER

LIES AT ANY PRICE: THE COMPLETE CASES OF GILLIAN HAZELTINE, VOLUME 1
GEORGE F. WORTS

HE RULES WHO CAN
ARTHUR GILCHRIST BRODEUR

THE HOUSE OF THE EGO: THE COMPLETE CABALISTIC CASES OF SEMI DUAL, VOLUME 3
J.U. GIESY AND JUNIUS B. SMITH

DEATH TO A TENOR
FRED MACISAAC

MURDER'S MASQUERADE: THE COMPLETE CASES OF MIKE & TRIXIE, VOLUME 1
T.T. FLYNN

THE LAND OF LIMPING LAW: THE COMPLETE CASES OF CALHOUN, VOLUME 1
EDWARD PARRISH WARE

COCKED DICE

THE COMPLETE CASES OF DAFFY DILL, VOLUME 1

RICHARD B. SALE

COVER BY

WALTER DE MARIS

POPULAR PUBLICATIONS · 2021

First Edition—2021

PUBLISHING HISTORY

"The Fifty Grand Brain" originally appeared in the November 3, 1934 issue of *Detective Fiction Weekly* magazine (Vol. 88, No. 6). Copyright © 1934 by The Frank A. Munsey Company. Copyright renewed © 1961 and assigned to Steeger Properties, LLC. All rights reserved.

"A Nose For News" originally appeared in the December 1, 1934 issue of *Detective Fiction Weekly* magazine (Vol. 89, No. 4). Copyright © 1934 by The Frank A. Munsey Company. Copyright renewed © 1962 and assigned to Steeger Properties, LLC. All rights reserved.

"The Ghost Wore Boots" originally appeared in the February 2, 1935 issue of *Detective Fiction Weekly* magazine (Vol. 91, No. 1). Copyright © 1935 by The Frank A. Munsey Company. Copyright renewed © 1962 and assigned to Steeger Properties, LLC. All rights reserved.

"The Mute One" originally appeared in the March 9, 1935 issue of *Detective Fiction Weekly* magazine (Vol. 91, No. 6). Copyright © 1935 by The Frank A. Munsey Company. Copyright renewed © 1962 and assigned to Steeger Properties, LLC. All rights reserved.

"Cocked Dice" originally appeared in the May 11, 1935 issue of *Detective Fiction Weekly* magazine (Vol. 93, No. 3). Copyright © 1935 by The Frank A. Munsey Company. Copyright renewed © 1962 and assigned to Steeger Properties, LLC. All rights reserved.

Visit argosymagazine.com for more books like this.

TABLE OF CONTENTS

THE FIFTY GRAND BRAIN

Was it a madman's jest, or a stroke of sinister genius? Why would anyone kidnap a dead man's brain?— That was what Daffy Dill wanted to know

1

BILL LATHAM'S HIDEAWAY CLUB was going full blast when I mushed in my tired huskies out of the frozen north of Broadway. The spot was getting a good play for so early in the evening—it was only midnight—and despite the snowstorm. Latham, I saw, was nothing more than a living grin at the chink of the coppers into the cash registers.

He saw me as I pushed past the lunatics by the check room, and he came over, looking like a Siamese cat, and stuck out his paw.

"Hello, Daffy," he said. "Come on in and have your poison on the house. It's a big night for me."

"I'll take you up on that, by God!" I said, shaking hands with him. "I'd better—while you're in the humor. Tomorrow you'll be squeezing my jeans if I don't pay up on my account."

"Aw, Daffy," Latham laughed, "don't be like that. You know me. I'm your pal!"

"Sure," I said. "I know." I made a cutting motion across my throat with my finger. He burst out laughing and slapped me hard on the shoulder. He sure was right.

"I like you, Daffy," he said. "You got a sense of humor."

I gave him a dead smile, and said in a soft sad voice: "Funny how the Old Man can't appreciate it."

"He down on you again?" Latham asked.

"No more than usual," I said. "He disallowed my swindle sheet this week. The hell of it is four bits of the eight bucks was legitimate. Ah, well!" I heaved a sigh. "Those are the breaks."

I glanced around the pub and took in the crowd.

I asked: "Anybody here, Bill? Come across—you know what I'm after."

Latham shrugged. "Pretty quiet, Daffy. Nice people mostly. You know." He seemed to recall something. "Oh, say—remember Gert Dodge?"

"Sure," I said. "The little blond doll."

"Well, she's over at the bar, filling her skin. She's crocked now, and in my business—even if I ain't a newshound—that means she's got a story on her chest."

"Thanks," I said, and left him. I went over to the bar where Shorty McInnis was sweating his weight off, shaking cocktails. Shorty was an old pal of mine. He had juggled beer mugs for years in the old Three Spot, my pet speak, before repeal. He winked at me when he saw me and wiped his beefy face. I winked back at him and pushed through the night-owls until I could park a foot on the brass rail.

"What'll you have?" Shorty asked, ignoring the soprano on my left who was yodeling for a Manhattan.

I said: "An Old-Fashioned, Shorty."

While he was throwing it together, I took a look around. Gert Dodge was on the far side of the bozo next to me on my left. Her eyes were sort of glazed, full of reddish veins and they looked as though she'd had a good sob. As I watched her, she tossed off the rest of a side-car, shuddered as she gulped it down. She was fully-oiled right then, and I didn't understand what kept her pins from buckling under her.

She said: "There's your yarn, Daffy"

SHORTY PASSED ME my drink. I flickered my thumb in Bill Latham's direction and said: "On the house tonight. The boss has gone gratis in a big way."

"O.K. with me, Daffy," Shorty said, taking the shrill soprano's bid.

I drank the Old-Fashioned slowly. While I did so, I noticed Gert Dodge giving me the eye but holding back as if she were debating something. I pretended not to see her and went on swallowing. It wasn't bad rye. In a few seconds, she came over and tugged on my sleeve.

"Hey!" she said thickly. "Ain't you Joe Dill of the *Morning Clarion?*"

"Daffy Dill to you, Gertie," I said. "How's tricks?"

She stumbled into the bar next to me, pushing the bozo aside, and rested her elbows on the rim and her face on her hands as she stared hard at me.

"Thought I rec'nized you," she said, doing her damnedest to keep her eyes open. "You're a leg-man, ain't you?"

"When I have news," I said dryly, "I am called a leg-man. When I have not, I am called numerous other and not so pleasant names. Why ask, Gertie? Could you hand me a yarn?"

She laughed harshly and leaned over the bar.

"Could I give you a yarn!" she exclaimed. She saw Shorty and he reminded her of liquor. She turned to me and pleaded: "Buy me a shot, Daffy!"

"Sure," I said with enthusiasm which plainly showed that Bill Latham was paying for my debauchery. "Name it."

"Same as you."

I snapped my fingers. "Shorty—another!" He got the signal. I turned back to Gert. "What this yarn you're insinuating?"

"It's a lulu," she said, shaking her head dully. "It's a natural, Daffy. Only—I'm the fall guy."

I perked up a little. You never can tell what a doll will carry around in her vacuum.

"Gwan," I scoffed. "Somebody's stole your man?"

"Honest, Daffy," she said, grabbing the Old-Fashioned that Shorty set down in front of her, "I'm not kidding. I said it was a lulu...."

"You're breaking my suspenders," I said. "Spill it, keed. You're in some jam. Maybe I can help you out."

She downed her drink in one gulp and turned around to me and grasped the lapels of my coat. She looked as though she were going to bawl.

"You couldn't help me," she whined. "Nobody can get me outa this rap!"

"Rap!" I said, surprised. I finished my drink quickly, set it down, and pulled her away from the crowd. "Let's get out of here, Gertie. Hand me the lowdown. What have you gotten into?"

I piloted her for the exit, planning on forcing some fresh air in her lungs before I had to carry her. She was too tight to protest. Outside, the snow in her face and the snap of the cold brought her out of it a bit and she walked more steadily.

"I'm losing patience, Gertie," I said, frowning. "Let me have it."

She looked at me in a silly way and then tapped my shoulder.

"Follow me," she said, just about audible. She wheeled and started to slither away through the snow.

"Where to?" I asked, catching her by the arm as she skidded into a hack driver, standing by the curb.

She said: "My place. I'll show you somethin'."

"You wouldn't fool me? There's a yarn?"

"Daffy," she said solemnly, raising her left hand with an effort. "S'help me. It's a lulu."

"Then for God's sake," I said, "let's get out of this Arctic and take a cab!"

"I only live around the corner."

I let her steer me into a dark cheap shack, hoping to hell she was sober enough to remember where she roomed. She seemed to know where she was heading. She took me up three flights of squeaking stairs through a hall that smelled as musty as my desk at the *Clarion* office. Finally, she reached the door she wanted. She took out a key and tried to find the lock where the hinges were.

"Ixnay," I said, taking it. "We can't waste the week. I'll open it."

I unlocked the door and gave her back the key. She turned the knob and threw the door open, beckoning me to come in. From where I stood, the room looked like any other flophouse. Rickety furniture was covered with cretonne that had fed the moths since the war. I followed her in and closed the door.

She said: "There's your yarn, Daffy," and pointed in the general direction of a black rocking chair on the other side of the room.

"God!" I exclaimed, gasping in spite of myself. Strength went out of me like liquor went into me. I felt weak and, at that particular moment, you could have blown me over with a whistle. There was a dead man sitting in the rocking chair.

2

AT FIRST I couldn't make out who it was. In the center of his face, all bluish and raised up into a welt like the bite of a giant mosquito, there was a bullet hole. The blood had leaked out of the hole and had plastered his features. Both of his hands were resting easily on the arms of the chair. He stared at us with open eyes.

I snapped: "Who's the stiff?"

Gertie had taken a seat on the sofa. She looked as though she were going to flop any moment. Her head dropped down into her hands. I went over and shook her.

"Who's the stiff?" I repeated sharply.

"Charlie Morelli," she replied like she was hypnotized.

"Morelli!" I said, peering at the features. "Not the same Morelli who was mixed up with Limpy Kassel's gang last fall! Not that undertaker—"

"That's him," Gertie said.

"Well, for God's sake," I said, "come across. Don't sit there getting sick at a time like this! I've got a beat here and you hold your head! When did you bump him?"

She leaped to her feet, her eyes blazing, and fell back drunkenly on the sofa.

"I didn' bump him!" she cried. "I didn', damn you!"

"So that's the typography," I murmured. She was telling the truth all right. I could see that. The police would see it, too, but they'd arrest her just the same. There wasn't anything else they could do. It was a gilt frame, and when Limpy Kassel put you in a picture, the State did the hanging inevitably.

I patted her on the shoulder.

"Listen, kid," I said, "it looks pretty tough. I think you're in for it, but I'll do my damnedest to yank you out. Now you've got to come clean. Tell me the works."

I put a cold damp cloth around her head and she began to talk.

"I came in at eleven-thirty," she said. "He was sittin' there like you see him. There was a rod on the floor."

I asked: "Where is it now?"

She pointed to the desk. I went over and looked at it without touching it. It was a .38 caliber pearl-handle Colt revolver.

"Who put it here?" I said.

"I did."

"Don't tell me you were fool enough to—"

"I couldn' help it!" she cried. "I was shot to pieces when I saw him like that. I picked up the rod without knowin' it. Then I felt sick. I saw the frame. I went down to the Hideaway and got drunk." She raised her head toward the corpse.

"Oh, Charlie!" she wailed.

I said quietly: "You sort of liked him, eh?"

"I was crazy about him!"

I thought hard for a couple of seconds. "Listen, kid, crying won't help. You're in a jam proper. The only way of getting out is to find the bird who really did it and lay it on. I know—" I added as she opened her mouth to speak.

"It was Kassel. Sure. But he and his lambs have cast-iron alibis for the evening. How about your own?"

Gert shook her head. "No alibi."

"Hell," I said. "That's just ducky. Got any idea why Morelli was bumped?"

"No," she answered. "But it was something he was working with Kassel on. I know that!" She flared as recollection surged through her. "Charlie told me only last night that Kassel was pulling a job that would net fifty grand. Charlie's split was ten."

"What was the job?"

"Don't know."

I sighed. "Haven't you any idea? Was it the coffin racket like they were pulling last spring?"

"I don't think so," she said, shaking her head. "It wasn't that. Kassel said something about a brain. That's all Charlie would tell me. The fifty grand brain."

"The fifty grand brain," I repeated after her thoughtfully. "If that ain't a natural for a head in twenty-four point! Now, listen, kid, you've got to sit tight. You'll have to take the rap and keep your mouth shut. Don't spill a thing, get it? Let yourself go, and I'll get you out of it if it's the last thing I do!"

"It may be the last thing," said a new voice from the door.

I wheeled around on my heel, startled. Detective-Sergeant Bill Hanley stood there, his fedora tipped back, overcoat buttoned up around his neck, and a toothpick between his lips.

"HELLO, POPPA," I said.

"Naughty boy," said Hanley. "Are you playing accessory after the fact?"

"Cut it out." I stared at him thoughtfully and then took a glance at the dead man. "How in hell did you know about this?" I asked.

He smiled, moving into the room, "Somebody phoned into headquarters and passed on the tip. Inspector Halloran sent me up. What's the dope, Daffy?"

I chortled. "A frame, Poppa. Look over the evidence yourself. Sure, you'll have to take Gertie in, but you'll know she didn't do it. Listen, who telephoned the tip?"

"We don't know," said Hanley. "We traced the call to a public booth in Gray's on 43rd Street."

"Gertie," I said, "they even nailed down the lid of your wooden kimono. Those boys didn't miss a trick. Well, look, Poppa. All you want to know is right here. I've got a story right under my beak and I'm going after it."

"I dunno," Hanley said. "Don't play me dirty, Daffy. You're not withholding—"

"I wish to God I were," I said, "But I'm clean. Gertie didn't bat this ball, Poppa. And finding out who did is going to be a big help in raising my pay. So long!"

He let me go. I was damn glad to get out of there without answering a lot of questions. But Bill Hanley knew me all right, and we had worked together on more cases than one. He was a nice enough guy, but—being a cop—he was too scrupulous, and he liked to be shown the why and wherefore of things on paper so that they added up to four. You know those kind. They annoy me.

After I reached Broadway again, I cut down towards 43rd Street past the Hideaway Club, whose business was steadily increasing. It was snowing harder, and the lights of the Paramount were in a funny sort of white haze. I reached 43rd and went into Gray's. Stubby Lewis was behind the drug counter.

"You're on the prowl," he grinned. "I can tell it by that gleam in your eye."

"That gleam in my eye is good," I said. "You oughta be a shamus, Stubby. Well, help me out. Was Limpy Kassel in here tonight?"

"About an hour ago," said Stubby. "My, my, Daffy, but you're getting up in the world. After big shots now, eh?"

"Did he telephone?" I asked.

"I wouldn't know. Say—he did something queer, though. He bought a stick of grease paint."

"So Limp's going to become an actor," I murmured. "What brand was it, Stubby?"

"Old man sallow," Stubby said. "Dan Furman and Blackie Shane were with him."

"They always are." I made a face. "Thanks, Stubby. I'll write your obit free some day in return."

"My pal!" he said.

3

I GRINNED AND went to the phone booths. They were full. I waited a second until a big lady finished her verbal jamboree and vacated the premises. Then I moved in, found a nickel somewhere in the desolate reaches of my pockets and called the office. Dinah Mason answered the call with a sweet: "Morning, *Clarion* office. Whom are you calling?"

Dinah was a nice kid, fresh out of college, and filled with the burning ambition to write the movie reviews. She had what it takes.

"Sweetheart," I said, "this is Daffy. Would you be so kind as to connect me with an imaginative rewrite man?"

"Hello, lunatic," Dinah said. "Don't tell me you've had a story trip across you?"

"Yea, verily," I said sadly. "It tripped across an Old-Fashioned. I didn't know you were on the night shift this week."

"It's not bad," Dinah said. "It saves me making excuses so's I won't have to go out with you."

"Give me a rewrite man," I barked, annoyed.

"He's all yours," she said, and she plugged me through to Bradley, who's a good one at sixty words a minute.

I gave him the yarn, telling him to play up the angle that Gertie might be innocent. I told him who made the arrest, and all the sanguinary details. But I skipped the part about Limpy Kassel, since the libel laws are unkind to innuendos.

When I had finished, Bradley said: "You ought to skip over to the Wagnall funeral parlors, Daffy. There's been some trouble over there. Speaking of Morelli reminded me of it. The Old Man sent Sam Lyons down with a picture snatcher."

"The Wagnall parlors?" I asked. "That's a classy layout, isn't it?"

"For fashionable corpses," said Bradley. "Some one attacked the caretaker tonight, or whatever the hell they call the bird left at the place. I don't know the all yet. Sammy hasn't called in."

"Where is it?"

"At 66th and Amsterdam."

"O.K.," I said. "And leave that Gert Dodge story open, Brad. There may be a follow-up that'll blow the town open."

"Don't flatter yourself," Brad said laconically.

I hung up, marveling at the nice people you don't meet in the newspaper racket. I went out into the snow again, feeling like Liza crossing the ice, and probably just as cold as she was too. I caught a trolley north to 59th Street and got off and walked the rest of the way to Central Park West.

When I reached the Wagnall Mortuary Parlors, there were two patrolmen standing out in front, blowing smoke rings with their breath, and swinging their nightsticks around meaningly. I ignored the nightsticks, but I had to show them my press card. I didn't know them, which is unusual for me, because I always know the most unimportant people.

Inside, Sam Lyons was waiting impatiently to get his

yarn from a wizened little fellow with a gray mustache who was still so scared he couldn't speak coherently.

Inspector Halloran, himself, was there, so I knew right off that the story would take a number two headline. Somehow, the fact that one undertaker had been bumped, and another attacked and beaten, all in the same night, impressed me. Morelli's establishment was a pretty poor one—a cheap setup for pauper corpses they fished out of the East River. Wagnall's was the ace of funeral parlors. I couldn't see how the two were connected—but it seemed queer just the same.

INSPECTOR HALLORAN LOOKED glad to see me. He came over with a peculiar glint in his eyes and said: "I didn't know you was carrying the torch for Gert Dodge, Daffy."

"Did Poppa Hanley tell you that?" I asked. "By God, I'll pun the pants off him in the story."

"I'm only kidding," said Inspector Halloran. "Bill phoned the bad news in, told me you'd been on the scene. Looks bad for that kid, Daffy. I know, I know! She didn't do it. I ain't been a cop all these years to see that. But my hands are tied. Why're you so interested?"

"Because there's a story," I said. "And it happens to be a story that'll save the kid's life. She was nerts about the corpse, Inspector."

"She was mighty broken up," Inspector Halloran said. "When Bill phoned—"

"*Caramba!*" Sammy Lyons exploded. "Is this a literary tea, gentlemen—or are you gonna make this guy talk? Lissen, chief, I'm only a hard-working reporter who'd like to be back in the warm seclusion of his office. I've been standing here for twenty minutes, waiting—"

"Skip it," said the Inspector. "How's he doin', Doc?"

He spoke to Dr. Emanuel Toomey, the assistant medical examiner of the bureau. I hadn't seen him. I waved to him.

"Hello, Daffy," Dr. Toomey said. "He had a pretty bad blow on the back of the skull, Inspector. Looked serious for a while, but it's finally resolved itself into just a bump like most of these things do. He can talk if you want him to."

"*I* want him to," said Sammy. "And make it snappy, chief. This corpse parlor bothers me."

Inspector Halloran went over to the injured man.

"Feelin' better?" he asked.

The man nodded, scared to death.

"What's your name?"

"Louis Vance."

"Well, Louis," said the Inspector, "let's hear what happened. When we got here, you were out cold right beside the casket there. One of your apprentices, that pimply kid there, found you and called in." He pointed to a terrified young fella with big eyes.

"I was on the night shift," Vance said. "Nothing to do but fix up a body. It's in the laboratory past that door." He nodded. "Suddenly, three men came in. They were masked and they had guns. They told me to keep quiet. One of the men attacked me. I bit him in the hand, but he cracked me on the head with his gun. That's all I know."

"What'd they take?" Sammy asked, scribbling.

"The place ain't been disturbed," said the young kid. "I looked all around and they didn't take anything."

"A wonder they didn't lift that nickel casket," I said.

"That's a silver casket," said Vance. "Fern Woodruf is in it. He was to be delivered tomorrow morning."

"Hi-de-hi," I caroled thoughtfully, walking over to the kimono and fingering it. "Fern Woodruf, eh? You people got the job of fixing him up?"

"Yes. And an honor too. There isn't a parlor in New York that's had as big a corpse as Woodruf to handle."

"Who's Woodruf?" asked Sammy.

"For God's sake," I exclaimed, "don't you ever read the papers? Fem Woodruf died yesterday—the passing of one of the world's greatest scientists—all America mourns its great loss—thousands—"

"I get it, I get it," Sammy said. "Come to think of it, I did see a squib on the obit page."

"A squib!" I said.

"Cut it out," said Inspector Halloran. "So you bit one of the birds in the hand, eh, Louis? Which hand?"

"The right one," Vance said promptly. "He carried the gun there."

"Bite him hard?"

Vance gritted his teeth, his eyes flashing. "I drew blood."

4

MEANWHILE, OVER BY the silver casket, I was doing some heavy thinking. A possibility struck me and I yipped loudly. Every one looked at me as though I were crazy. Inspector Halloran sighed.

"What's the brainstorm, Daffy?" he asked.

I said: "Seems mighty queer, chief, that three mugs would knock out Vance, here, and then not touch anything in the place. Unless Vance had enemies."

Vance said: "I have none."

"Good," I said. "Then that means the three bad boys came here after something, knocked out Vance so's he wouldn't see what they were doing, and departed."

"I don't get it," said Inspector Halloran.

"Ever hear of body-snatching?" I asked. "You know—grabbing a famous corpse, holding it for ransom under threats of maltreating it if the money were not paid?"

"Hot damn!" said Sammy.

"Nuts," said the Inspector. "The casket's still here."

"Open it," I said, "and see if Woodruf is still *inside* of it. That's more to the point."

"Hell," said the Inspector, "we can't go busting open caskets just to—"

"It's very simple to do, Inspector," said Vance. "I can remove the head cover in a second. I'll do it."

He went to the casket and we all crowded around expectantly. Vance unscrewed two bolts near the head and heaved on the head plate covering the upper half of the casket. It came up heavily. He slowly lifted it off.

"Hey!" I exclaimed sharply. *"It ain't Woodruf!"*

Vance whispered: "My God!" and dropped the head plate to the floor, narrowly missing his own corns. I never felt a tighter sense of dread than I did in that room. All of us gaped at the casket.

There was a corpse in it—but not Fern Woodruf. Not the angular bearded outlines of the scientist's face. Instead, the body of a young girl reposed on the silks. There was a red welt around her neck and I knew right off that this girl had committed suicide. She was dressed poorly and her face was dirty, hair flowing down awkwardly on her shoulders.

"A body-snatch!" said Inspector Halloran. "I ain't had one in the department in six years, at least!"

Me, I was putting three and three together and having them make nine. Somehow, although it was my own idea in the beginning, the body-snatch was out. It looked to me as though the three yeggs had transplanted the girl in Woodruf's casket with the idea of having her buried in Woodruf's place. If that were done, they couldn't make a claim that they had the real body without an exhumation. It didn't click, you see.

I began to piece it together a bit, too, and see how Charlie Morelli tied into the thing. Morelli, with his cheap undertaking establishment on—Henry Street, wasn't it?—might have gotten hold of this girl's body after a suicide. Unidentified, or secreted, Morelli could have held her for this job—to be transplanted in Woodruf's casket when the switch was pulled.

But why had Morelli been bumped? I thought of the fifty grand job Gertie had spoken of. Morelli's cut was supposed to have been ten grand. If Limpy Kassel had engineered the holocaust, and Morelli were through being useful, Limpy's love of money would have prompted him to bump off Morelli, make Gertie take the rap, and thereby save himself and his angels ten thousand dollars.

"I'M GOING HOME," I said. "I've got to think. Sammy—you'd better phone your story in. Tell them to add it to the Gert Dodge story and give us both by-lines on it. Tell them to hold both yarns open for another add."

"You got something?" Sammy asked, looking like a vulture on top of a tower of silence.

"Lissen, Daffy," Inspector Halloran said, "don't play me dirty. If you've got a lead—"

"Inspector," I said, "I'm clean, I swear. I've got an idea but I've got to work it myself. I'll let your department in on the ending—if there is an ending, so wipe your face."

"That's your word, Daffy," said the Inspector. "I'm letting you go on that."

I borrowed a sawbuck from Sammy—it was like lifting an elephant with one hand—and took a cab outside the Wagnall parlors for my own hideout, a quartet of modest rooms on East 90th Street, for which, believe it or not, forty-four bucks of my hard-earned pay went out every month.

There was a funny sort of quirk going around in my head all the way home. I kept trying to remember what it was Fern Woodruf had to do with me. Because he did have something to do with me. Sometime, somewhere in the past, I had hooked my fist into a fact about Woodruf which I thought would have made a good chunk of fiction—that was when I was young and foolish and thought that newspaper men actually wrote all the fiction they said they planned to write.

I arrived at my spot, my memory still virginal as far as that quirk went. I paid the hack driver off with a part of Sammy's sawbuck and went upstairs. I went rummaging through my desk drawers as soon as I got in, looking for the damn-fool note-book I used to keep, filled with news-rag clippings which would have made story plots. Finally I found it and went through it.

I said: "Eureka!" and slammed my knee hard. The clip was in it. That was worth a drink. I mixed a rickey in the kitchen, brought it back to the desk, and slowly drank it as I read the clipping.

It said in effect, that the American Academy of something or other had paid Fem Woodruf twenty-five thousand dollars for his brain, to be delivered to them upon his death and after—of course—autopsy. But the clipping went further. This American Academy was taking no chances. They had insured Woodruf's brain with the Amalgamated Insurance Company for one hundred grand!

How long ago this had happened was a mystery, since the clipping held no date. But I remembered that I had collected those ideas for plots sometime within the last five years. It didn't make any difference really.

Well, the whole set-up was as plain as Bill Hanley's face right then and there. Limpy Kassel—unless I was all wrong—had lifted Woodruf's corpse to get his fingers on that brain. Morelli had been double-crossed with Gert to take the neat rap. Then, after the whole thing was a boil, Limpy would demand fifty grand from the insurance company. Or else. The else, in this case, would be simply that he would destroy the brain and cause them a loss of twice fifty grand, which they would have to pay to the American Academy which had insured the brain.

Neat but not gaudy, eh? You had to hand it to Kassel—he saw swell possibilities in the mess and he played his hand the moment Woodruf died, which by the way, was a natural, from pneumonia. I saw the same possibilities years before, only I would have made fifty fish from the yarn—if I had ever written it—and Kassel stood to make fifty grand.

5

I FINISHED THE rickey and picked up the telephone and called headquarters. Some grizzled old blowhard answered in a voice that sounded like the foghorn of the Berengaria at sea.

"Daffy Dill of the *Clarion,*" I said, "wants to know if there has been any reports on the finding of a headless corpse in the last two hours."

"No," the blowhard growled, "but they will find one if you ask questions like that around. You're screwy!"

"It's a pleasure," I said and hung up after giving him a prolonged and reverberating bird.

I called the *Clarion* office right away. Dinah Mason's honey voice dripped over the wire with her usual opening.

I sang: *"Dinah, is there anyone finer—?"*

"Alas and alack!" she sighed. "Are you in again?"

"Yet, you mean," I said. "Will you marry me?"

She said: "No!" emphatically.

"In that case," I said, "let's get down to business. Has anyone reported finding a headless corpse within the last two hours?"

I heard her gasp and mutter "Damn," under her breath with all the tautness and fervor of a veteran.

"Daffy?" she cried, "are you a spiritualist?"

"Never mind the wisecracks," I said seriously. "They've found one then?"

"Ten minutes ago," Dinah said. "Down on Fourteenth Street in a blind alley. Body of a man, stark nude, head lopped off clumsily. Body dead for two days at least. It was embalmed. Scars, appendix and double hernia operation. Description—"

"Skip it, skip it," I said. "You've told me all I had to know. Give me Brad for rewrite."

"He's gone out for a sandwich," Dinah said. "Let me take it, Daffy. Please! Sammy just phone in about the fight at the Wagnall parlors. The Old Man is all excited. He's breaking down the first page. I want to do—"

"O.K.," I said. "Did you telephone headquarters about the corpse?"

"Yes."

"Then get this. That body was Fern Woodruf's. The corpse which was in Woodruf's casket at Wagnall's was taken from Morelli's undertaking spot earlier in the evening. Go light on that. I haven't checked yet."

"I've got it," Dinah said. I could hear the keys of her typewriter clacking merrily. "But give me the rest. Why the missing head? What's the motivation? Who did it? What kind of a newspaper man are you?"

The door of my apartment closed behind me with a slam. I turned around, startled. Blackie Shane stood there. His face seemed to convey the impression that it was not a friendly call, and when I saw the gun in his hand, I knew it was not.

I said swiftly: "Dinah—Blackie Shane just walked into my place without an invitation. There's an evil gleam in his eye and a .45 pistol in his mitt. Just thought you'd like to know in case he should get careless and give way to his feelings which—plainly—are to bump me off."

"Daffy!" Dinah said. "Are you mad?"

"I'll call you back," I said, and slid the receiver back on the hook. I turned around and looked at Blackie Shane. "So Limpy is on the warpath!"

HE HAD PIGGISH eyes and I didn't like them at all. He wasn't intelligent enough to realize that if anything happened to me now, Dinah would get him cold for first degree murder. He might plug me and worry about that later. He stared at the telephone.

"That won't help you," he said.

"That won't help *you,*" I said. "I'm doing very well, thank you. But if I should suddenly develop a chronic case of bullet wound, then you are definitely on the ice, Blackie. If you get what I mean. So put away the shooting iron and parlay."

He sat down but he didn't put the rod away. He kept fingering it nervously, training it on the pit of my stomach.

"You're a nosey guy," he said in a nasty way.

"I get around," I said. "That's my job. Limpy doesn't like it, eh?"

"Not much he doesn't," Blackie replied. "He sent me up to cook you."

"Tch-tch!" I clucked. "What a pity!"

My ticker was slamming against my lungs and pounding blood through me so hard, I could feel a blue vein sticking straight out on the left side of my temple. The muzzle of his rod looked like some dinosaur's mouth. I felt cramped, tight, and raw. I didn't like it.

He looked at me for a long time, staring, without saying a word. Silence beat on my ears like thunder. Finally, I said: "Well?"

"I dunno," he said. "I dunno what to do now." He got to his feet and waved the pistol. "Get away from that phone."

I rose and walked across the room, wishing to hell there was a gun or bomb or something under the cushions on the sofa. But there wasn't, of course, and I sat down on them.

He called a number, still holding the gun on me.

"Limpy?" he asked. "I'm in Dill's apartment. He was on the phone when I got here and he told that frill at the *Clarion* that I was going to bump him. What do I do?" He listened to his boss for a few seconds, nodding. He looked pleased and I felt worse at the sight of his expression. "O.K.," he said. "That's swell, Limpy. I'll handle it."

He hung up and called the *Clarion* office.

"I wanta speak to a doll named Dinah," he said. Apparently Dinah was on the other end for he went right on. "You know Joe Dill? Well, unless you go right away to 142 East Fourteenth Street, he's gonna be knocked off, get it? And if you tell the cops or anyone else, we'll give him the slug anyway. Now step on it, sister, and—"

I hurtled out of the sofa towards Shane, crying: "Dinah!"

But Blackie Shane had anticipated my rashness. He hung up and turned to me in a slow way. Just as I reached him, he clubbed me with the rod.

I went out like a light and didn't come to until lots later. When I finally opened my eyes, my head was ringing with bells, and I saw I was in a car heading down Madison Avenue.

"Easy does it," Blackie said, jamming the pistol into my

ribs. I was washed out at that moment. He didn't have to warn me.

At Fourteenth Street, he called the hack driver over to the curb, paid off, and then walked me down Fourteenth, prodding me meaningly with the gun. And if you don't think he would have let me have it right there—if I had tried anything—you're crazy. Blackie certainly had a wrinkle in his brain. That's why Limpy used him as torpedo-man.

At 142, we went in and ascended the stairs until we reached the door of Limpy Kassel's hideout. When I went in, I wondered if I ever would come out. Plainly, I wasn't supposed to, nor was Dinah, once she reached it.

6

SHE WAS ALREADY there, I saw, talking to Limpy, himself, a short man with a club foot. His face was gnarled with lines, but he had pleasant eyes just the same.

"Hello, Daffy," he said. "Sorry to see you here."

"Are you all right, Daffy?" Dinah asked anxiously.

"Sure," I said, eyes narrowed. "Spill it, Limpy. What's the idea of pulling the kid in?"

"Just a precaution," Limpy smiled. His face tightened with a soundless snap. "Now, listen, Daffy, you've been poking your nose into the Morelli bump-off and you've been playing hunches on the Wagnall fracas tonight. I don't like it. 'Cause that happens to concern me. I want you to kill any story you've written which might cast some doubt as to whether Gert Dodge killed Morelli or not. Otherwise, I'll have Blackie and Dan Furman put the slug on both of you."

"I'm killing no story," I said. "And lay off the girl. What's she got to do with it?"

"She knows Blackie came to your place," Limpy said. "Tough, but if you go, she's got to go, or we don't cover ourselves. You ought to know that, Daffy. Better play ball."

"And suppose," I said, "that I'd play ball and then cross you?"

"Ever hear of Dynamite Thompson?" Limpy asked.

"Who hasn't?" I stalled, biting my lip thoughtfully. "The Detroit babyface is big news."

"If I should ever be crossed," Limpy said, "Dynamite Thompson would fix up you and your doll very nicely. I've already wired him that you're in on our play."

I kept rubbing my nose. Dinah noticed it. She got up and wandered around the room aimlessly. She finally got behind Blackie, staring at the ceiling and wringing her hands as though she was unnerved.

"Well," Limpy said, watching me rub my nose, "yes or no?"

If he knew me, he would have realized that my rubbing my nose was a pretty good sign of "No!" Dinah realized it. I always do that just before a scrap. She anticipated me and, son-of-a-gun, if she hadn't gone and planted herself next to the light switch on the wall.

"Limpy," I said, "you can all go to hell!"

Dinah clicked out the light switch at the same second. I heard Blackie Shane cry out as I stepped back and tried to grab him to place a haymaker on his jaw. I felt him on the floor.

Dinah snapped: "Get his gun! I tripped him!"

I fell on him, pounding the back of his neck with my fists. I felt him go sort of limp and figured one of the rabbits had taken him. But he was stiff conscious. His right hand came up with the gun. I grabbed it and snapped a mean twist on it. Blackie emitted an awful scream and dropped the .45.

I found it and yanked Blackie half up from the floor to cover me. Dan Furman was framed against the background of a window, which showed him up plainly. He kept calling, "Limpy? Limpy?"

"Let 'em have it!" Limp snarled. "To hell with Shane—the fool!"

ORANGE FLASHES SLICED the darkness, and the room was quickly filled with acrid smoke and roaring thunder. Slugs whined over my head—I was kneeling on the floor—and slammed thuddingly into the plaster of the wall behind me.

"Dinah!" I called, frightened for her.

"Nuts!" she hissed in my ear. "I'm on the floor. Give it to them, Daffy!"

Heartened that she was O.K., I drew a bead on Dan Furman, who didn't know the window showed him up. I fired twice and he buckled up like a folding chair and laid down. The .45 kicked hard in my hand, snapping back and hitting me on the side of the face.

Limpy was in complete darkness. I saw his gun fire as he let loose at the flashes of my rod. One slug whizzed by my left ear like a big bee. The other hit Blackie Shane, whom I was using as a shield. That bullet had impetus, because it knocked Shane back at me, and nearly threw my body over backwards.

I fired twice again at Limpy but I must have missed. He came right back at me blazing away for all hell. He was getting accurate, for he hit Shane again with both slugs. Shane was dead as hell. I could feel that as I clung to him.

I heard Limpy's club-foot pounding on the floor. He had stopped shooting. A door opened and closed.

"He's taking a powder!" I said to Dinah. "Stay here!"

I went after him, gun swinging in my hand. I tore

through the door, searching the other room in the darkness for some sign. It was as black as pitch and I couldn't see a thing.

And then the lights flashed on.

It was Limpy who had turned them. He caught me unawares. I had a short glimpse of him, a revolver sticking out in his right hand, a black valise in his left.

He fired at me.

The bullet clipped me in the shoulder with a powerful blow which spun me around and crashed me back against the door. I couldn't feel a thing, it was just like a punch.

I lost my balance and started to fall, my mind still perfectly clear. I could see Limpy plain as day. There was a satisfied grin on his face and his gun was raised for a final shot. Somehow, I couldn't lift the .45 in my hand.

Simultaneously, a chattering series of cracks rang out from *outside* of the room. The window pane was shattered into splinters as fistfuls of slugs zoomed into the room and caught Kassel amidships, bunching together like a baseball.

They socked him over on his heels and flat on his back like lightning, and after he hit, he never even twitched.

I was sitting on the floor, feeling stupid, when I saw the stock of a Thompson sub-machine gun break through the rest of the jagged window pane and smash it down. A man finally squeezed through, still carrying the sub-machine gun. He stared at Limpy's corpse for a second, then glanced at me. It was Bill Hanley.

"How're you doin'?" he asked with a grin.

"Poppa!" I said. "Will you tell me how in the seven hells you happened—"

Dinah Mason came in from the other room at that moment.

"You all right, sweetheart?" she asked me.

"I'm nicked," I said. "It can't be bad. It doesn't hurt."

"Lemme take a look," said Hanley.

He peeled off my coat and opened my shirt. I watched him with interest. There was a bullet crease on my left side, extending under my armpit. Close, but no cigar. It wasn't even bleeding, but it looked raw.

"YOU'RE O.K.," HANLEY said after a few minutes.

"Thanks, Poppa," I said.

"Now would you mind telling me—"

"Dinah called me after Kassel called her," Hanley said. "She's a smart girl, Daffy. Any other doll would have taken Kassel at his word and kept her mouth shut. Then both of you would have been bumped. She's unorthodox. She actually asked the cops to cooperate."

"I'll be damned," I said. I glanced at Dinah. She was looking at Kassel's hands.

"I can't find it," she said. "Maybe we've made a mistake."

"Woodruff's head?" I asked. "It's in the black bag."

"No, no," Dinah said. "Vance at Wagnall's said he bit his attacker's hand. None of these three men have any mark at all. And when Sammy phoned in, he said Vance said that blood was drawn. Look—there isn't a mark on Kassel's paws. And none on Furman's and Shane's."

I winked as I put on my coat. "You didn't know that Lumpy was aiming to become an actor, Dinah."

"I don't get you," she said.

"Grease paint, grease paint," I said. "Lumpy bought a

stick of sallow grease paint at Gray's tonight after he and his angels socked Vance at the Wagnall parlors."

"Oh," said Dinah. "He covered up the scar with grease paint and made the skin look natural. But which one of them has the scar?"

"Lumpy," I said. "The other two have pinkish skin on their hands. Lumpy is the sallow one. Rub his right paw and see."

She rubbed and the bite which Vance had inflicted stood out like a sore thumb. It was a mean thing, that bite. Vance had sure sunk his canines into Lumpy.

I got to my feet, feeling a little dizzy.

"Well," I said, "let's get to the office. We've got this yarn to write. It's past deadline for the first edition right now." I sighed. "Just think—I've saved somebody fifty grand. And I'll have to fight like hell with the Old Man over my dear old swindle sheet because I took a cab tonight. Ah, well!"

"Daffy," said Bill Hanley, "how'd you like to sorta put an O. Henry finish to that yarn in the *Clarion?*"

"Poppa's turned editor," I said, waving a reproving finger. "But I'll take it. What's the finish?"

"Lumpy was rooked," said Hanley, "just like you. When we told Mrs. Woodruf that her husband's body was taken, she gave us the story about the insured brain. That was what you were after, no?"

"Sure," I said. "It's safe and sound, right in that black bag."

"It's safe and sound," Hanley said, "but not in the black bag. That's only Woodruf's head. You see, Vance removed the brain before he embalmed the body, according to instructions received from Mrs. Woodruf. It's at the academy that wanted it."

"What the hell!" I said. "Then why didn't Vance say so when I was there and save me a bullet wound?"

" 'Cause you yourself said it was body-snatch for ransom. He never thought they were trying to extort by holding—supposedly—Woodruf's brain."

"That's all right, lunatic," Dinah said, patting my cheek. "You always mean well."

Well, when you read it in the *Clarion,* it made a good story just the same, even if I didn't get a raise.

A NOSE FOR NEWS

Was the Tipsy Huntington Heiress Keeping Her Weird Vow to Kidnap Herself—or Was Gangland Paying a Debt with Her Blood?—Here Is a Thrilling Adventure of Daffy Dill

1

THE TELEPHONE ON my desk rang, so I stopped banging out the lead of the double suicide story I had just covered and answered it. It was Dinah Mason, who is decidedly bad for my heart. She was the reception girl for the *Chronicle,* and she had buzzed me from the outer office.

"Hello, Garbo," I said.

"Listen, Daffy," she said in a low voice, "a lunatic just went by here yelling your name. He looks angry. I couldn't stop him."

"Thanks for the warning, gal," I said. "But I'm not on the spot for anything—as far as I can recall."

"O.K." She sounded funereal. "He sure looks mad."

She hung up as did I, and no sooner had I shoved the telephone back where it belonged than the door to the city room burst open and the maniac stalked in.

He was a little guy, well dressed, with a black derby perched on the top of his skull. He was waving a home edition of the *Chronicle* in his right hand like a red flag. He kept saying "Which one of you is Joe Dill? Which one of you pencil-pushers is Joe Dill?"

I kept my mouth shut, waiting for him to reach me before identifying myself, and hoping that by that time some of the hot blood would have cooled off.

The rest of the staff, in the tradition, kept their pans a

perfect blank. If I wanted to make myself known, that was my business alone.

But just then Harry Lyons, the rat of our sheet, who had been sore at me since I got his job, gave me a dirty look and pointed at me. His biggest aspiration, you see, was to find me flat on my face with a knife between my shoulder blades. He said: "Here he is, mister. Meet Daffy Dill, the world's worst newspaper man."

I snapped: "Button your lip, Lyons!"

But he saw trouble for me. He smirked broadly, got up, and took the maniac by the arm. He pulled the guy right over to my desk and put a chair there for him.

"Here," he said, motioning at me, "is the Cyrano de Bergerac of the newspaper racket All nose—no news! Ha-ha!"

"Ha-ha!" I said sadly, surveying Lyons' face for the exact spot where I was going to hang a haymaker very shortly. I picked his eye. That was the most ignominious spot.

"Are you Joe Dill?" the maniac asked loudly.

"I am," I said, "Joe Dill. Sit down, my fran. What's wrong?"

"What's *wrong?*" he bellowed with new fervor, slapping his copy of the home edition on my desk and hurling the chair aside. "He asks me what's wrong. *Du lieber Gott!*" I got more and more puzzled. "Mr. Dill," he said sibilantly, "do you know who I am, *hein?*"

I said: "You've got me there, mister."

"I am Adolph," he went on. "Adolph, America's premier chef! Do you know what you have done?"

"Adolph?" I echoed. "Well, I'll be damned! Adolph, the chef of the Grenada Hotel? Well, what in hell are you sore

The bullet went over my back with an angry whine

about? Didn't you see that swell feature I wrote about you in the second section today?"

"Swell feature," Adolph moaned. "Mr, Dill, you should be arrested! *Verdamnt*—you should never be allowed to write again. You have libeled me! You have been malicious! I will sue this damn paper to heaven!"

He turned stoically to Lyons and asked with dignity: "Where is the editor?"

"Right this way," Lyons said, smiling sweetly at me. "I'll take you right in. Don't blame you a bit. Newspaper men shouldn't libel their readers. You're absolutely right. This way."

When he had gone in the vague direction of the Old Man's office I grabbed a stray copy of the *Chronicle* and hurriedly thumbed through it to my story, which had made a big enough hit with the Old Man to net me a by-line. I read it through carefully. Near the end I groaned. It went like this:

"Adolph was famous long before he entered the cuisine of the Grenada Hotel. For ten years before the war, he was the most famous of all the crooks of Vienna."

Libel? It was dynamite, fuse lighted and all! I had meant to say that he was the most famous *cook* in all Vienna. But somehow my typewriter must have slipped in that wandering r while I was pounding the keys. I groaned. I locked my desk, got up, and found my hat and coat. I knew right then that I had joined the legion of the unemployed, but somehow that word *crook* still rankled me. I was damn positive that I hadn't written *crook* for *cook*. And if I had—why hadn't the copyreader picked it up and fixed it? Suspicion grew, and in five short minutes I realized that Harry Lyons, C.T. (Cut-Throat), had pulled a sandy on me. So I waited for him.

IN A LITTLE while, Adolph came out of the Old Man's office with a happy expression on his face—as though he had just seen my corpse. He sneered a sneer at me and left the city room. No sooner had he gone out than Lyons came to my desk.

"Why, hello, Daffy," he said. "The Old Man wants to see you right away."

"You don't say," I said. "And some one wants to see you right away too."

"Who is it?" he asked.

"Your favorite doctor," I said.

With that I let him have a short sweet haymaker right under his eye, which spot I had chosen previously. There was a pleasant crunch. His teeth clicked together neatly. His eyes closed with a snap you could hear on West Street. He went down and—out.

McGuire, the sports editor, looked up from the story he was writing about Lou Gehrig and yawned: "Nice punch, Daffy. Better see the Old Man anyway. He may have mercy on your soul."

"Thanks, Mac," I said. "I'll see him."

I went to the Old Man's office and knocked. Then I opened the door and stuck my head in, weaving in case he started to throw things.

"Come in here, Daffy," the Old Man ordered. "Sit down a second."

"On the level?"

"Why, Daffy, did I ever—"

"O.K.," I growled. "Ixnay on the pathos. Let's get it over."

He nodded and I sat down.

"In the first place," he said, "you are fired."

"I knew that," I said.

"Listen, Daffy," the Old Man said suddenly. "I hate like hell to do it, but I've got a boss too, the guy who publishes this sheet. I couldn't let you stay."

"I know, I know."

"I had to settle with that frocked cook for one grand. He wouldn't take a cent less for release of that libel." The Old Man shrugged. "I have to fire you. Can't do anything else. But I wanted to speak to you about those gambling expose articles you've been writing, the ones you left with me for safety."

"They're mine," I said. "I did them on my own time."

"I know it," he said. "But I want them. They'll blow Cantrey's graft organization wide open when I break them.

"Now I'll tell you what I'll do. I'll keep 'em here. You go out and run into the prize scoopy of the year. It'll have to be an exclusive. Then I'll just be forced to hire you again, over the publisher's head, to get your yarn. And all will be serene once more."

"You mean," I said, "that I've got to scoop the A.P., the U.P., the Metropolitan News Service and every other rag in this city to get my job back?"

"Yeah."

I sighed. "The day of miracles is past, my fran."

The Old Man shrugged. "You'll have to do it. I can't take you back otherwise. I've got to protect myself. I want you. You're a good newspaper man, Daffy. And I want that gambling expose too. Make a try anyhow. You've got thirty bucks due on salary. How about it?"

"Slave-driver," I said, "I will try. I'll do my damnedest, even if I have to steal or murder myself. So long. When you see this intelligent phiz again it will hold in its mind the greatest circulation yarn in days."

I went out. I felt enthusiastic and fine. The Old Man was a prince. He liked me—or my gambling story. When I reached the street, I went limp. Where in hell could you get a scoop in a modem newspaper day like this? I began to feel down. So I took the subway up to Times Square, which is my happy hunting ground. And then I went to the *Hot Spot Club* to drown my sorrows for awhile.

2

THE *HOT SPOT* is on West Forty-third, and it is owned by Mike Cantrey, alias the Brain. Cantrey headed just about every racket on the main stem. No murder, beering or bootlegging. Not crude stuff like that. He just took suckers. He ran machines, gambling houses, spots like this one, which were blinds for his crooked wheels in the rear. And it was Cantrey I had written my exposé about.

I went in and took a seat by myself in one of the oaken stalls. A waiter came over and looked questioningly at me. I said: "An Old-Fashioned, garsong, as ever."

While I was waiting for him I lighted a cigarette. A shadow fell across my table. I looked up. A girl was standing in front of my stall. She had corn-hair, a smooth-looker, and was dressed like the Queen of Sheba.

"I know you," she said, pointing.

She was a little bit tight and she was holding a rye highball. I thought I'd seen her before somewhere, but I played safe. I said: "You've got the better of me, Garbo."

"You're Daffy Dill," she said.

"Right the first time," I said.

"You're a reporter on the *Chronicle.*"

"Wrong there," I said sadly. "I was a reporter on the *Chronicle.* I just lost my job. That's why my tears are staining my best shirt. Sit down and put up your hair and have a good cry with me. Who are you?"

"Tough," she said—about the job, and then added: "I'm Clare Gordon." I didn't look bright. "You know—Pemberton Gordon's daughter. You interviewed him at the house last week on the N.R.A. He's in the cloak and suit end as administrator."

"Hell, yes!" I said, shaking hands with the gel. "But I didn't see you there or I would have stayed longer." I surveyed her. "You make pretty good copy yourself. Been in any more scrapes lately? I haven't seen a yarn about you since you forced down the police plane when it tried to get you for stunting over the city."

She made a face. "That was a jam. They cracked up in landing. I've reformed. Dad played hell with me on that one."

The waiter brought my Old-Fashioned.

"Have one?" I asked.

"Sure," she said. "Thanks."

"Another," I told the waiter. He left.

"How'd you lose your job?"

I said: "I happened to have a guy in the office who hates my nerve. He had my job but he couldn't deliver. They promoted me to his forty fish a week and he's been sore at me ever since. He fixed me into a libelous story. Changed one word and got the paper in a jam. It looked as though I'd written it—and so I am fired."

"Tsk, tsk," she said, shaking her head. "Bad, bad. Daffy, am I a pal?"

"My fran," I said, "I have known you for years."

"You help me out," Clare said, "and I'll get you back your job."

"Why not?" I said. "Consider yourself helped."

She handed me a slip of paper. It had a list of figures on it which added up to five grand. "Know what that is?"

"I.O.U.s, probably," I said. "Been playing the wheel?"

"Not me," she said. "I'm not that dumb. But my brother has and he's in a real spot. Dad's cracked down on him lately. Won't give him money. Dick was playing the wheel here at Cantrey's. He lost. He gave them an I.O.U. each time. Now they want to collect. They're going to go to dad and I know it'll get Dick disowned or something. I told him I'd fix it up. I saw the Brain. He said no."

"Five grand," I mused. "O.K., girlie. You sit here and devour your drink. I'll be right back."

I GOT UP and went to the back door. Rigo, the Brain's right-hand man peered out at me through the barred door.

"Oh, it's you," he said, and opened up. I went in.

The tables were all getting a good play, even for daytime. Suckers were plunking down the coppers and having them swept away without a bit of return, but they kept right at it. I asked Rigo: "Where's the Brain?"

"In his office," Rigo said. He was a little guy with black hair, black mustachio, and squinty eyes. "Want to see him?"

"Yeah."

He took me in. The Brain was sitting behind his desk, smoking a cigar. Luke Terk was sitting with him. Luke was the Brain's muscle man when customers were broken-armed about paying up. Rigo closed the door behind us.

"Hello, Daffy," said the Brain. "How's tricks?"

"Fair," I said. "I want to ask a favor."

"Anything for a pal," said the Brain, smiling, and I shivered because I knew damn well he would have liked to have had my throat slit. "What is it?"

"There's a guy named Richard Gordon," I said. "A good pal of mine. He owes you five grand."

"That's right."

"Tear up his I.O.U.," I said. "He's a personal friend, you see. He didn't know your wheels were crooked."

Luke Terk jumped around and stared at me. "Listen, birdie, button your lip or—"

"Why, Luke!" the Brain said. "Don't speak like that. Daffy's my best friend, aren't you, Daffy?"

"How about it?" I asked.

"Afraid the answer's no," the Brain said. "Five grand is five grand."

"I see," I said. "Mind if I use your phone?"

"Go ahead."

I called the Old Man at the *Chronicle.* The three buzzards watched me carefully. The Old Man said irascibly: "Yeah."

"Chief," I said, "this is Daffy Dill. I'm at the Hot Spot seeing Mike Cantrey. He just refused to do a favor for me. Don't you think it was about time the *Chronicle* ran that series of articles exposing his crooked gambling joints all over the city?"

"Hell, no!" the Old Man said. "You haven't finished them up yet."

"Fine," I said. "I'll tell him he can read all about it in tomorrow's editions then."

"Wait a second," the Brain said.

"I get you," said the Old Man. "You're baiting him. Keep talking if you want. I'll play along from this end."

"Nice going, chief," I said. "But wait a second." I put my hand over the mouthpiece and asked: "What is it?"

The Brain studied me. "Is that on the level?"

"You bet your sweet life it is!"

"It can't hurt me. I've got the political boys greased."

"Yeah," I said, "but you haven't got the public greased. You take their money and they'll be sore when they read about it. They'll put the blame for any time they've ever been gypped on you. Maybe there'll be a Federal inquiry. And in two months there's an election coming up. The people won't elect your political boys unless they clean you out."

Luke Terk snapped: "This is one guy we oughta cook, Brain."

"Let me do it!" Rigo growled.

"Boys, boys!" I said. "Don't be silly. You don't kill a reporter who has just written an exposé of you. That adds murder to the other crimes."

The Brain said: "He's right, you lugs. Call off your dogs, Daffy. It's a deal. I'll give you the I.O.U."

"Chief," I said into the phone, "it's all off. You'll have to hold those articles for another favor. So long."

I hung up. The Brain opened his desk, took out a note, handed it to me.

"I'm on the short end," he said. "You've still got those articles for publication. How much for them?"

"I'm not blackmailing," I said.

"You mean you'll run them sometime anyhow?"

"Yeah," I said. "But you'll have time to get your affairs together and start a new racket, Brain. Gambling's dead from now on."

Luke Terk growled: "Get outta here, you rat, before I forget myself and blast you."

I got out.

3

CLARE GORDON HAD finished her Old-Fashioned when I went back to the stall. She was a little tighter. She laughed at me and asked: "How'd you make out?"

I handed her the I.O.U. "Is this your brother's signature?"

She nodded. "That's it."

"Then you're all set." I took out a match and burned the note. "Tell him he's in the clear. Also tell him to lay off crooked joints. Now, how about my job?"

"That's right," she said. "I told you I'd get it back. I've got a swell plan. I'm going to be kidnaped."

"What?" I cried.

"Sure. I'm going to be kidnaped tomorrow night at eight o'clock. By aeroplane."

Rigo went by the stall at that moment.

"Shh," I said. "Not so loud. Now, what in hell is this?"

"I just figured it out," she said, "sitting here. You write my folks a threatening letter, saying I've been kidnaped and that the ransom—"

I sighed. "Did you ever hear of the Lindbergh Law?"

"Sure, but what's the difference? All right then. I'll write my own letter. I'll say that I've been kidnaped and the ransom is two hundred thousand. I'll name you as go-between. Then I'll take off from home in my plane tomorrow at eight P.M. and fly up to Binneybunk, Maine, where dad has a cabin. It'll be deserted there now. After a week or two, while you bask in the publicity of go-between and your paper cries for your services, I'll come back and tell a wild story."

"You're hopped," I said. "You're staggering. Forget it. I wouldn't go in on a plan like that for money."

"But I want to help you!"

"Help me? You want me to become a lifer in a Federal jug!"

Clare wrinkled her nose. "All right. But you can't stop *me* from doing it. And I'll write the ransom note and still name you as go-between."

"I'll blow up the story."

"And they'll pinch you for conspiracy or something. I'm telling you, Daffy. Tomorrow at eight P.M. I hop off for Maine and kidnap myself. Them's the kind words that gets back your job."

Well, she meant what she said. I was sitting in my apartment the next night around eight thirty, bemoaning the lack of scoops in this dazzling world. I had had a hard day trying to find a story which would yank back my job, but no luck. My nose simply wasn't in the news. I was washed up. Then my telephone rang.

I answered it with: "Your nickel!"

It was my heart, Dinah Mason. She thrust aside the usual sentimental amenities and said: "Daffy, hell's broken loose!"

"Somebody bomb the office?" I asked cheerfully.

"It's Clare Gordon," Dinah said. "She's been kidnaped. Half an hour ago. She was taking off from her father's estate out near Huntington, Long Island. Three men jumped her. At least that's what the chauffeur says. The snatchers piled into the plane and they all took off for points unknown."

I chuckled. "Damn the gel! Any other fine points?"

"There was a ransom note left behind. It names *you* as go-between! The bulls have been here for you. They're on their way up there now! The Old Man is frantic, trying to find you. The last place we looked was home. You're seldom there."

"Listen, Dinah," I said, "don't get excited. The Gordon skirt framed this whole thing. I'll tell the Old Man when I see him. It was put-up."

"Are you sure, Daffy? It doesn't look like a frame."

"It's a frame, my chickadee," I said. "Forget it. Who's covering for the paper?"

"Harry Lyons."

"Oh me, oh my," I gloated. "What glorious fun! Abyssinia, my hourglass. Look me up in Atlanta."

I HUNG UP, threw on my hat and coat and took a powder before the police reached my place. I wasn't any too soon either. They roared up the street to the door, sirens going, just as I went down the block. I caught a cab, said: "Headquarters, Mac," and settled back on the cushions to enjoy the ride, which cost me seventy-five cents when I finally paid off in front of the Centre Street building at the other end.

I went up to see Captain George Shane, who, I figured, would be in charge of the case, even if it had taken place on Long Island. They centralize things like kidnapings, because one man has to stand in with the Federal authorities when they come searching. Inspector Halloran and

Sergeant Bill Hanley of the Homicide Squad were both on the out in this snatch.

I was right. Captain Shane was my man. Every newshound in the city was outside his door, pounding on it, trying to get in and get hold of some facts. A cop—I recognized him as Curly Newton—was pushing them aside. In the midst of the holocaust I saw Harry Lyons. He had a bad eye where I had brushed him off. I said: "Gentlemen of the Press!"

There was sudden silence. They stopped pushing and turned around. Lyons yelled: "Daffy Dill!" and that started it. I forgot for a moment that I had been named go-between in Clare Gordon's screwy ransom note. I was a public figure in the case. They mobbed me for a statement while Curly Newton tore into Captain Shane's office. In a second or two, before I could say a word, Newton came out again and dragged me through the mob into Shane's office. He closed the door and I liked the quiet for a change.

Captain Shane was pacing the floor in front of Pemberton Gordon, Clare's father. He recognized me easily since I had interviewed him for the paper only the week before, as Clare had said.

There were two other men in the room too. They were Federal operatives. I could see it as plain as day.

"Daffy," said Captain Shane. "You heard what's happened?"

I nodded.

"You heard you've been named go-between?"

I nodded again, looking at Pemberton Gordon's face. He was scared to death. His hands were trembling. I could see a vein in his temple throbbing like hell. I felt sorry for him.

"Listen, Captain," I said, "I just heard about it and I came right down to blow it up. It's a fake."

"A *what?*"

"A fake, a pushover, sandy. It's a frame. The kid did it on purpose to help me get my job back."

Captain Shane stared at me. "Daffy, are you on the level?"

"You know me, Captain," I said. "I don't lie to you."

"Then start talking," he snapped. "Let's hear this one."

I talked and told him all that had happened, how I'd done the gel a favor (I didn't say what it was because her old man was there) and how she wanted to do something for me. I told how she said she'd kidnap herself, name me as the go-between so's I'd get the job back. Shane listened without saying anything, just nodding now and then, but I saw that Pemberton Gordon was regarding me with the kind of a look he'd give Frankenstein's monster. And the Federal dicks were giving me the kind of eye which meant a rubber hose. I prayed.

When I had finished, Captain Shane shook his head.

"Daffy," he said, "it sounds fishy. I've known you a long time and all that, but it sounds fishy. I don't like to say it—but it does. Now come clean."

"Chief," I said shortly, "that's clean. I wouldn't fool you."

"He's one of the gang!" Gordon exclaimed. "I know he's one of the gang. That's why he was named as go-between. He knows where Clare is! I want him arrested!"

One of the Feds said: "Don't worry about that none."

"Wait a second," I said. "Take it easy, boys. I'm telling the God's honest truth." I was sweating like a soda glass. "The girl is up at her father's cabin at Binneybunk, Maine. Why don't you check on that and see if I'm right."

Shane nodded. "That's sound."

"We'll do that little thing," one of the Feds snapped.

"Meanwhile," said the other, "you're being detained as a material witness or suspicious character or anything you'd like. Put him in the can, Captain."

"That's what I'll have to do, Daffy," said Shane. "Sorry."

"O.K., chief," I said. "Just so we clear the thing up I told that scatterbrained frill I wasn't in on it. She said that wouldn't stop her."

"We'll wire the Binneybunk sheriff," said Captain Shane. "Sit tight in the jug. You'll know in an hour."

4

THEY PUT ME in a cell. The minutes took a hell of a long time to pass. I smoked. I got to smoking so much I used a whole half pack of cigarettes and my tongue felt like the Russian army had walked across it with bayonets fixed. I kept sweating and my hands were trembling. I don't know why, but I felt damned uneasy.

At ten o'clock Captain Shane came to see me.

"Did they find her?" I asked.

"Daffy," he said slowly, "I hate like hell to do this. But Pemberton Gordon just swore out a warrant for your arrest. You're charged with aiding in the kidnaping of one Clare Gordon, and anything you say from now on can be used against you. They're setting your bail at twenty-five grand."

"Twenty-five grand!" I yelled. "Arrest? Chief, for God's sake, listen. The girl—"

"She wasn't there," Captain Shane said. "The cabin hadn't been opened since Gordon was up at Binneybunk last summer."

I wilted. "Oh," I said. "Oh, thanks." I was croaking, not talking. "Thanks, chief. I—I guess I'm in a jam. Do me a favor, will you?"

"Sure," he said.

"Get me some cigs, please?"

"Sure. Anything else?"

"Telephone—telephone the Old Man. Tell him I want to see him."

Captain Shane shook his head. "No need of that, Daffy. The Old Man's here. He wants to see you."

"Can he?"

Captain Shane shrugged. "O.K., I guess. But only for five minutes."

"Thanks," I nodded. I felt better somehow. The sweating stopped. The suspense was killed. I knew where I stood. He went away. In a few seconds the Old Man puffed up to my cell and stared at me.

"Daffy, you old jailbird," he said, "when I told you to go scoopy, I didn't say get a life sentence doing it. Is it a story?"

"It's a story," I said. "But I'm the fall guy."

He looked me straight in the eye.

"Tell me one thing," he said. "One thing, Daffy. You're clean on this thing?"

I said: "I'm clean, chief."

"Good." He chuckled. "Then spill it."

I spilled it, the whole damn thing, and he listened, taking in every news angle it had. When I finished he remarked: "It's a lulu, all right. It'll make us dust off the type we used for the Armistice. But you can write it? If I get a machine up here, can you write that yarn? Can you—" He stopped and glanced warily at me. "Wait a second. If you—hell's bells! The girl wasn't at the Maine cabin. That means she's really been snatched!"

I nodded.

"Daffy," he said, watching my face, "do you know who did it?"

"I've got a good idea," I said.

The Old Man got pale. He paced back and forth a few minutes. Then he called: "Be right back," and left. I felt for a cigarette, but I didn't have any. Captain Shane came along and slipped me a pack. I paid him for them, they hadn't taken my belongings yet. "Thanks," I said. The Old Man showed up just at that instant.

"You're free, Daffy," he said. "I called up Kennril. He said that with the yarn behind it the *Chronicle* was going to post bond for your bail. That's legal. All O.K., Captain?"

"Hell, yes," Shane said. "The *Chronicle* is good for twenty-five grand. Have you signed the papers?"

"No, but I will now. Let the boy out."

"Not till the bond is posted."

THEY WENT OFF and fixed that business up while I jiggled on pins and needles. Every minute was precious. After an awfully long wait the turnkey came and let me out. The Old Man and Shane were waiting for me in Shane's office. Shane gave me a card, in case other bulls tried to put the bite on me.

"Judas," I said to the Old Man, "thanks! Thanks for everything! I'll never—"

"Wait a second," he said. "You've got to earn that bond. Go out and after them, Daffy. And try to break it right for the noon edition."

"Say," asked Shane suspiciously, "does he know the snatchers?"

"I don't know a thing," I said. "See my lawyer. O.K. I'm on my way." I shook hands with the Old Man "I mean it, chief. Thanks."

"Get to hell out of here," the Old Man snapped.

I had a gun permit for a .32 Colt, but I never carried the

rod. I figured I need it tonight, so I took a cab uptown to my place. There was a cop out front. I didn't want trouble. I went in the back way and upstairs. I found the rod all right, primed and ready to go. I slipped it in my coat pocket and went out the back way. Then I headed for the main stem, crossed it, and went into the Hot Spot. I called a waiter. "Is the Brain in?"

"No." The reply was surly.

"Rigo? Luke Terk?"

"Naw, they're all out."

"O.K.," I said. I went out and turned into the back alley. I knew if any one of the three came they'd go into the Brain's office the back way. I took up a spot in the shadows and waited with my right hand wrapped fondly around my gun.

I waited about fifteen minutes. It was ten after eleven by the Paramount clock. I heard footsteps come along the street. I ducked back farther into the shadows. A man turned into the alley. He was all alone. I recognized him. Rigo, with his short-stepped gait. I let the Colt go. I reached in my pocket and took out my penknife and snapped open the blade.

Rigo was careful. He took a good look around himself, but it was damn dark where I stood. He missed me. He aimed for the side door of the *Hot Spot,* and for one second he turned his back to me.

I jumped out of the shadows, threw my left arm around his neck and jabbed the knife into his back, just enough for him to feel the cold steel.

"Hello, Rigo," I said. "Nice seeing you again."

He was breathing hard. He gasped: "Who is it?"

"Daffy Dill," I said. "An old friend." I sneaked my

Daffy Dill

left hand into his shoulder holster and put his gun in my pocket. "Don't move, you rat," I snapped, "or I'll give you the length of this blade." He didn't move. He asked:

"What're you after, Dill?"

"Clare Gordon," I answered, "and the boys who snatched her."

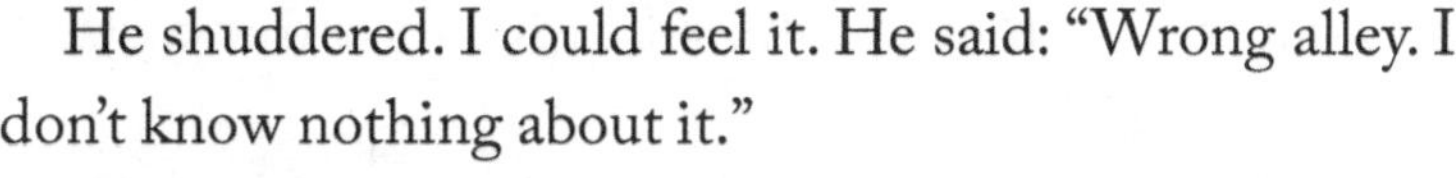

He shuddered. I could feel it. He said: "Wrong alley. I don't know nothing about it."

"Listen, you crumby little bum," I snapped, "come clean. I'm not kidding now. The Brain engineered this. You overheard the gel say she was going to stage a fake. You were taking it out on her because I got that I.O.U. of her brother's back. That and the fact that I wrote those gambling expose articles which will blow your business to hell. You needed a new racket, and the Brain chose this one."

"You're crazy!" he said.

"Rigo," I said coldly, "where is she?"

"I tell you I don't know."

I took the knife and cut him deep across the back of the neck. The blood started running down over his shirt.

"Rigo," I said, "you're going to tell me or I'll cut your head off. Come clean. Where is she?"

"I tell you I don't—know!" His voice was shrill and he was breathing hard from the pain. That pup was scared to death.

"Want another cut?" I asked.

"Leave me alone! For God's sake, leave me alone. I don't know anything about it, I told you—"

I cut him again on the back of the neck, deeper this time. He winced and began to half sob from the pain. "For God's sake, Dill, are you crazy? Leave me alone!"

"Where is she?"

"I don't—"

I put the edge of the blade across the front of his throat. I tightened it there.

"Rigo," I said, "I'm going to tell you a little secret. I'm out on bail. I'm charged with Clare Gordon's snatch. If I don't find out from you where she is I'm due for either a death sentence or a lifer term."

"I don't know where she is!"

"I haven't got much to lose, Rigo," I said coldly. I pressed the knife harder. "Your jugular vein is right there. If you don't spill her location in ten seconds I'm going to slice your throat wide open and let you bleed to death."

"That's murder, Dill!"

"Sure," I said. "But what have I got to lose. Your ten seconds are up. Here goes. So long, Rigo."

I cut him slightly. He half screamed and tried to break away from me. I listened to his shrill words as he got hysterical with terror. "She's at the Brain's place! She's at the Brain's place!"

"Take it easy," I said, easing up on the blade. "What do you mean?"

"The Brain's place!" he babbled. "Uptown. Ritz Towers! The Brain's penthouse!"

It's funny how fear will make a guy squeal on his own mother. I kept the knife on him but just enough for him to feel it. "How'd she get there?" I asked. "You snatched her when she was taking off in her plane from Huntington, Long Island!"

"The Brain and Luke Terk engineered the snatch over there! I waited up at Yonkers with a speedboat!"

"Who piloted?"

"Cantrey! The Brain!" He was gasping.

"What then?"

"Cantrey set the crate down in the Hudson. He had flares."

"Was it an amphibian?"

"Yeah. Land and water. We broke the pontoons and let the crate sink. Then we came down the river in the speed-boat. I had left the Brain's Lincoln by the Fifty-seventh Street pier. We tied up the boat and got in the car. We took the Gordon doll up to the Brain's place. I came back here to make things look right."

"Thanks," I said, "for the interesting lecture."

5

I TOOK OUT his rod and cracked him on the skull with it. He went out like a light and sagged to the alley floor. I figured him cold for at least an hour. I ran down the street to a cigar store, stuck a nickel in a telephone and called Dinah Mason.

"Hello?" she said.

"It's Daffy," I said.

"Darling," she said, "what's happened to you? The Old Man got word that you were being held in connection—"

"Listen, my little rattlesnake," I said. "I just put the bite on Rigo. You know Rigo—the Brain's right or left hand. I forget which. Anyway, he opened up and squealed beautifully. Now get this, because I'm on my way. Clare Gordon is being held captive at Mike Cantrey's penthouse apartment at the Ritz Towers. In case they should bury me before you see me again, tell some one else that pertinent information and write the story along with my obit."

"Check," she said. "Be careful, you lunatic. Don't get killed just when I've got you that way about me."

"I'm not going to try," I said, "but you never can tell."

I hung up and hooked a cab for uptown. We made the Ritz Towers in nothing flat. I paid off the driver—four bits, it was—and I went in. I found out how the Brain got Clare up there without suspicion. He had a private elevator to his place. I said I wanted to see him. They made a call upstairs.

"The answer," said the desk clerk, "is no. Mr. Cantrey is seeing no one tonight."

"Tell him," I said, "it's about some gambling articles a fellow once wrote."

"He'll see you," the desk clerk said after relaying the kind words. "Take that elevator."

I took it. It was a non-stop at that time of night and we went up so fast I felt as though I'd left my stomach on the first floor. I got out. I didn't have any plan. I was just planning on inspiration. There was only two of them. I knew that. The Brain didn't go in for mobs.

I rang the bell. Luke Terk opened the door.

"Hello, rat," he said.

I went in. He had a gun in his right hand. With the other, as I passed him, he frisked me. He found my Colt and made me take it out. "Drop it on the floor." I dropped it. I felt sort of empty. I had counted on that gun for a jam. "O.K.," Luke Terk said then. "Go on in. One funny move and I give it to you."

His voice was cold and low. He meant it.

THE BRAIN WAS sitting in the living room. It was a swanky spot, all furnished modernistic, the way the furniture looks when you wake up with the jitters and a bad hangover. He smiled at me in a self-satisfied way. I had a feeling I was in for it.

"Come to the point," he said. "Never mind the gambling stories stall."

"All right," I said. "You snatched Clare Gordon. The gel's here. I want her."

"You want the moon," said the Brain softly.

"Maybe so," I said. "But I want her."

"She ain't here."

I laughed nervously. "You're stalling now, Cantrey. I hopped Rigo in an alley. He squealed."

"I know," the Brain said. "You cut him with your knife. Sorta nasty trick, wasn't it, Daffy?"

I felt icy. "So he came to and called you?"

"Yeah. He's got a tough skull. Sorta nasty, wasn't it?"

"Not for a rat like Rigo," I said. "He had it coming. I don't like snatchers, Brain."

"My, my!" Luke Terk exclaimed. "He don't like snatchers." His voice went taut. "Well, I don't like guys with knives, Dill!"

"He had it coming."

"And so have you," said the Brain. "Ever had your feet burned with matches? Ever had needles stuck through your skin? We do that with welchers, Daffy. I think we'll stretch a point. Maybe you ain't a welcher. But you was pretty rough on Rigo. And Rigo is a pal of mine, see?"

"You're running a sandy," I said. "You can't scare me now. Go ahead, torture me. Then bump me off. The Feds are still after Clare Gordon. They don't miss out on their cases, Brain."

"She ain't here."

"Sure," I said, "she's flew away with a little birdie. Don't kid me. She's in the Ritz Towers somewhere. Rigo squealed once. He'll squeal again."

"The Feds don't carve guys' throats," snapped Luke Terk.

"Rigo's O.K.," said the Brain. "But you're not, Daffy.

You're washed out. You've poked that big nose of yours into trouble this time."

"Into news," I said. "A nose for news."

"You stuck it into a coffin," said Luke Terk. "Only this time the lid's on it and you can't pull out."

I waited for a second and didn't say anything. They had the drop on me coming and going and there wasn't a thing I could do except bluff and stall a little.

"I want Clare Gordon," I said.

"Nuts," Luke Terk growled. "O.K., chief?"

The Brain nodded. "O.K., Luke. Give it to him. And make it hurt."

Luke Terk jabbed his gun in my ribs. "Get over to that sofa," he said. "And lie down."

I started for the sofa. Simultaneously, there was a hell of a racket in the streets below. We were up some sixteen floors, but we could hear the police sirens as plain as day. They were screaming and I could hear the cars grinding up to the curb.

The gun in my ribs loosened. Luke Terk tensed and turned.

"Chief," he snapped. "Bulls! This lug must've tipped them off!"

"Take it easy," the Brain said. "Maybe they're not for us."

"They're for you," I said. "I tipped them."

Luke Terk cried: "Chief—what'll we do with him?"

"Take him along!" the Brain said. "You take him down where the doll is. I'll stay here and parley with the cops. You—"

Now was the time for all good men to come to the aid of their party. I spun around, swinging with my right. It was a good swing, but I hit without a target, since Luke Terk and his rod were behind me. I heard the Brain yell. I missed Terk's chin and hit him on the left shoulder.

6

THE PUNCH HURT my fist. It hit solidly. Luke Terk went down, but I had fired the arm so hard I fell right on top of him. I hit him again as we sprawled. This time I caught him on the beak. It spouted blood. He tried to bring his gun hand up.

The Brain yelled again. Then there was a shot. The bullet went over my back with an angry whine. If you don't think slugs make noise, you want to get that close to one of them. I shot out my foot and smashed it down on Luke Terk's hand. Terk yelled with pain and his fingers shot open. The gun dropped to the rug.

Another shot from the Brain. The rug in front of Terk's head jumped as the slug dug into the floor.

"For God's sake, chief!" Terk screamed. "Go easy!"

I dove for the gun Terk had dropped, keeping low and not giving a damn whether the Brain hit me or not. I got into the spirit of the thing. I reached the gun, picked it up. I wheeled on my belly, firing twice. The slugs never went near the Brain, but they scared him. He let go another wild shot at me that missed by feet and then tore out of the room into the hall. I could hear the front door slam.

Luke Terk was struggling to his feet. On my knees, I covered him with the gun. He was reaching into his coat pocket.

"Cut it!" I snapped.

He must have figured that I was bluffing. He kept right on into his pocket. I saw his hand come out. He had the .32 pistol in it, the rod he had taken from me in the entrance hall when he frisked me.

"Cut it," I snapped again.

He raised it for a shot. I yanked the trigger of his own gun. It jumped in my hand. It made an awful racket. He fell over backwards as though I had hit him with a sledge-hammer. The .32 flew up into the air and smacked a picture on the wall, knocking the glass pane to bits.

I got to my feet and looked at him. There was a hole in his right lung. His chest was bleeding. He was conscious, his eyes were open and his lips kept moving as though he were trying to say something. Nothing came out. He'd live. Sawbones can fix up wounds like that one.

I stepped over him and started for the entrance hall. At the same time the front door burst open. I turned around and ran for the bedroom, the gun still in my hand. The window there was opened. I shut the window after me and started down the fire escape. I knew if the police caught me there with Luke Terk wounded and no Clare Gordon to show for it I would be in a worse jam than ever. I had to get the Brain and the gel.

I went down two floors on the fire escape when I heard the window of the Brain's bedroom open. I hugged the wall of the building and stopped moving. Then I heard him say: "No one down there," and he closed the window again. It was Captain Shane.

I took a breather and wondered what in hell to do. I was marooned on the fire escape. The only chance I had of getting off it and trailing the Brain was by going through a window, into an apartment, and then out into the hall and down, dodging cops all the way. It was a small chance, but the only one. And it wouldn't do to have Luke's gun on me.

Glancing down into the street, I saw it was pretty deserted. This was the side of the hotel, not the front where the cops were. I heaved the gun out and away. I could hear it hit, just dully.

I tried the window in front of me. It was locked. Swearing softly, I went down another flight of the fire escape and tried the next one. It was unlocked. I opened it softly. The shade was down. It was dark green. I pushed it aside and stepped into the room. The lights were out. It was dark as hell. I stood there for a few seconds, trying to adjust my eyes. There wasn't a sound in the room. But in the one adjoining I could hear some one walking around. I started across the room. A floor board creaked. I stopped, stiffened.

Suddenly I gasped. The bed in the room was squealing loudly as some one moved on the springs.

"Take it easy," I whispered. "I'm a friend. I won't hurt you." I felt like a fool, but what else was there to say under circumstances like that?

The bed squeaked more and more. Some one was bouncing up and down on it. I had a hunch. I walked over to it and struck a match.

Just like I thought. There lay Clare Gordon....

SHE WAS BOUND with thick adhesive tape both on her ankles and her arms. Her hands were spread out flat against each other and taped. There was a wad of tape across her mouth. Two ropes stretched across her body and under the bed, prevented her from rolling off.

She looked at me pleadingly. The match went out. I lighted another and went to work on the tape over her mouth, motioning her to keep quiet when she could speak. I pulled off the tape. They had stuck a lemon in her mouth. I took it out. The first thing she said was: "Judas Priest I I'm nearly dead!"

"Shh," I said.

I took off the rest of the tape and she sat up. She had to rub her legs to bring back the circulation. I said: "Well, you sure did it."

"Thank you, my fran," she said, grinning. She had what it takes. You couldn't keep her down. "They jumped me. They must have overheard me at the *Hot Spot* yesterday. Just when I was taking off they jumped me and flew off with me in the plane. Landed the plane in some river. Then a speedboat. Finally a car. Then here."

"Were you upstairs first?" I asked.

"Uh-huh. But somebody named Rigo telephoned and that oyster, Luke Terk, took me down here for safety. Thanks for saving me. It was good fun while it lasted, but I was getting stiff. How's your job? Get it back yet?"

"Listen, hair-brain," I said, "you're not saved yet. In the next room there's mug with a gun and he's just aching to kill me."

"What are you going to do then?" she asked.

I shrugged ruefully. "I don't know. I haven't a rod. Damn it!" I sat down on the bed a second. "Guess we'd better go up by the fire escape. The cops are up there."

"That's safe and sound," she said.

"Only you sound disappointed."

"I am. I'd like to get the Brain myself. It'd make a better news story for the *Chronicle.*"

"Then get him. Pick up a chair or something. Get behind the door. I'll yell help or something. He'll come in."

"Wahoo," I said, "that's an idea." Picking up a brass candlestick from the mantel, I went over behind the door. "Let go in your best soprano," I said, "but make it muffled, like your gag has worked off."

"Help! Help! Save me!" she half moaned.

Next door there was a strident curse. Heavy footsteps pounded across the floor. The door flew open.

"Shut your mouth, damn you," the Brain greeted, "or I'll cook you right now!"

Clare had nerve. She repeated: "Help! Help!"

HE CAME IN. There was a gun in his hand. The light from the other room fell square on his head. It was all I needed. I brought the candlestick down with a swish. He half turned, firing his gun just once. Then he flopped over cold and pieces of plaster from the ceiling caromed onto my hat. I snapped on the lights.

"My hero," Clare grinned.

"My God!" I sighed, sitting down. "What a night…" I paused, a brilliant thought pervading my struggling mind. "Listen, heiress," I said, "your old man had me arrested. Now I saved your brother five grand, didn't I?"

"You did."

"Do you think, then, your old man would have any objections to a five grand pay-off out of court?"

"Out of court?"

"Sure, instead of defending himself against my suit for false arrest."

"Daffy Dill!" she exclaimed, laughing, "it's a lulu. It'll do my heart good to see him sign your check!"

The door was being knocked down. I let them knock it. I was too tired, and cops have nervous trigger fingers anyway. In a few seconds Captain Shane, the two Feds, and half the police force came in.

"There's your package," I said. "And here's the wrapper-upper."

Captain Shane grinned. "That cleans you, Daffy. Thanks. Your better-half called me up after your tip-off."

"Did you hear the shot in here?"

"Yeah. That's what brought us in."

I sighed. "Where's a telephone?"

"Wait a second," said Shane.

"What in hell happened? Spill it."

"Uh-uh," I said, shaking my head.

"See the patient."

"How about it, Miss Gordon?" Shane asked.

"You can read the exclusive story," Clare said, "in tomorrow's edition of the *Chronicle*."

"Listen—" Captain Shane roared.

"Hello, Dinah?" I said in the telephone.

"Howdy, my cherub," Dinah said. "All serene and sound?"

"Not serene," I replied, listening to Shane, "but quite sound."

"Good," said Dinah. "So what?"

"Get out the cold cuts," I said, "and the beer and potato salad. Daffy's on his way up to see you."

THE GHOST WORE BOOTS

Real Lead Bullets Came Out of the Gun of the Ghost That Forced Daffy Dill to Aid Its Supernatural Crime

1

WHEN I EASED into the Old Man's office he tipped back his green eyeshade and asked, "Daffy, did you ever hear of Wilson Quayne?"

I sighed. "Did I ever hear of Abraham Lincoln? Of course I have. Quayne's the steel magnate. You're Satan himself. And I'm Daffy Dill, who's had a hard day and is going home to date Dinah Mason. What is this, chief, a game?"

"You're going," said the Old Man, "out to Spuyten Duyvil to Wilson Quayne's castle after a story."

"You're going," I said, "to the bughouse."

The Old Man grinned. "I mean it, Daffy."

"What's the yarn about?" I groaned.

"A ghost."

"Ha-ha," I said sorrowfully. "What kind of a ghost?"

"A special kind. He was wearing boots and carrying an old Colt six-gun. You know—one of those grave-scratchers that Wild Bill used to make Injuns bite dust with."

"Who called in?"

"Now there," said the Old Man, "is the story! Van Lamont called."

"I know only one Van Lamont," I said, "and he tries to act, outside of being a first-class skunk and thinking he's Hollywood's gift to Woman."

"One and the same," nodded the Old Man. "He's one of Quayne's guests. And the others are Majorie Culpepper and Ian Norman. Names, Daffy, all names! And names make newspapers!"

"Just what happened?"

The Old Man shrugged. "Don't know. Inspector Halloran tipped me off that Lamont had called from Quayne's to say that they had all seen a ghost and that the shade was none other than old Major Culpepper himself. Halloran's sending Bill Hanley out to check."

"Listen, chief," I said, "Dinah's a swell girl and besides Shakespeare used the last shade when he struck Banquo in 'Macbeth.'"

"Don't you get the setup, Daffy?" The Old Man was in earnest. "Here's a famous steel man—Quayne. A notorious actor—Lamont. Here's Majorie Culpepper, who heads her father's munitions company with Ian Norman managing president. They all say they've seen Majorie's dead poppa! Is that a yarn?"

I got up. "Okay," I said.

I went back to my desk in the city room. I picked up the telephone and called Dinah Mason—who is bad for my bloodstream. Dinah is a sort of receptionist on the *Chronicle.* She's got platinum blond hair and starry eyes and every time I see her, I go Spanish and I hear the tinkle of wedding bells.

She opened up with: "Your nickel. Broadcast!"

"The date is off, my hourglass," I said sadly. "The Old Man is sending me out to No Man's Land to cover a story. So I'll see you tomorrow, my little cupcake, and no two-timing."

"Veddy well," she said, just like that, and hung up.

I sighed disconsolately and trudged down the stair of the *Chronicle* building to West Street where I hailed an ambitious hack-driver. "Head north up the Drive," I told him, "and don't stop until we hit Alaska."

WE'D BEEN RIDING about an hour when the driver turned around and tapped on the dividing window.

"Are yuh sure this is right?" he asked hollowly.

"Sure I'm sure."

"Well," he said, "I guess you know."

"Why the question?"

"Nothin'," he answered. "Only—this is the loneliest damn country I ever been in. Spooky as hell!" He shivered. "Where are we, anyhow? Up near Bear Mountain?"

"Be yourself," I said. "You're still on the twenty-four buck isle of Manhattan. And there's my stop down the block where those big stone cairns are sticking out."

"Thank God," he said, and slued into the curb.

I opened the door and got out. Then I walked up the long circular drive to Quayne's castle. The grounds were dark. There weren't any shadows because there wasn't any moon. I shivered at the bite of the sharp river wind and trotted up the stone staircase which fronted the drive. After banging the big brass knocker a couple of times, I waited, listening to the low whine of the wind as it came around the corner of the house.

The door opened. A little majordomo stood there, looking a trifle startled.

"Yes?" he asked.

"Holmes," I said, "is the name. Sherlock Holmes of the homicide bureau. Inspector Halloran sent me."

I felt an icy tingle shoot down my spine

"A-about the ghost?" he faltered.

"About the ghost," I nodded.

"Come in," he said. "Mr. Quayne is in the library. I'll tell—"

A voice broke out irascibly from a pair of double doors to the left of the hall:

"Boggs! Boggs! Who the devil is it?"

A tall, thin man stepped through the doors. He was in a tux and he looked immaculate. His hair was absolutely white. He wore a monocle in his left eye. He stared at me. Behind him I saw Bill Hanley's good-natured pan come into focus and grin at me.

"Who is it?" Wilson Quayne repeated sharply. "Don't stand there shaking, Boggs!"

"It's—a—Mr. Holmes, sir," said Boggs. "Mr. Sherlock Holmes from headquarters."

"Don't be an ass," Quayne said. He turned to me. "What

nonsense is this? Who are you and what's your business here?"

"Dill's my handle," I replied. "Daffy Dill."

"A detective?"

"A reporter."

"My God!" he exclaimed. "Get out of here! I'll not be made a fool of by any—"

"Take is easy," I said. "I'm not making a fool out of anyone. The yam is public now. You called the cops."

"But it sounds crazy," said Quayne, horrified. "People will think that we were all drunk, or—"

"I know this guy," Hanley told him. "He ain't a bad egg, Mr. Quayne. Play square with him and he'll handle that yarn right."

"Sure," I said. "Hell, Mr. Quayne, I'm no sensationalist. All I want is the story—if there *is* one."

He considered this and then nodded.

"Come inside. I was just explaining it to Sergeant Hanley here. And Boggs—in the future remember that Sherlock Holmes is a character—not an entity!"

We went into the library and I said, "Let's have it from the beginning."

"Very well," Quayne clipped in that precise style of his. "We were sitting here after dinner at about seven-thirty. I was right where I am. Majorie was in the center there and Van Lamont was on the other side of her."

"Majorie Culpepper, that is?"

"Yes. Ian Norman had been drinking before dinner. He felt tipsy. I suggested that he lie down on that sofa over there. He did so, and fell asleep. The rest of us were sitting here, talking. The lights were all down and only this fire illumined the room. At about a quarter of eight, I saw something whitish out of the corner of my eye. I turned—"

"Yeah?" I asked eagerly.

"Right over there," Quayne said, "directly in front of the tapestry, I saw him."

"Who?"

"Major Culpepper," Quayne said. "I'm as sure as death. He was right there—white and hazy and nebulous. As I stared at him—in some horror I must confess—he walked across the room towards the sofa where Norman was asleep. He was dressed in that riding habit of his and he had on his boots—"

"Halloran mentioned a gun," I said.

"Yes." Quayne nodded; he paled too. "In his right hand, he held that famous single action Colt of his. It was a .31, a relic of the boom days of the West. He carried it with him always. Eccentric on the point."

"I know," I said. "I had to interview him once when Culpepper Munitions was up before the Senate for inquiry. I remember him twirling the grave-scratcher around his finger. I was scared it'd go off."

"Well," said Quayne, "the last thing he did was aim that gun at Norman. Then he disappeared just like a flash! That's my story and I'll swear to it!"

"Did Majorie Culpepper see him?" I asked.

2

"YES. NATURALLY WHEN I saw the thing, I gasped. It really was a terrible sight, gentlemen. She and Lamont saw it, too. She screamed and Lamont leaped to his feet. Then it vanished!" He shook his head. "Oh, it was the Major all right. I'd recognize that handle-bar mustache of his anywhere."

"You don't believe it was a spook?" Hanley asked gruffly.

"I—don't—know," Quayne said slowly. "It was nothing human. It was something I could see through. It was a man I know is dead, a man whose cold flesh I felt in his coffin."

"I can't arrest a ghost," grunted Hanley. "I think you've been tricked, Mr. Quayne."

"Maybe so," said Quayne. "But if I was, then I can't trust my own eyes any more. Nor my mind. It was Culpepper. I don't know if he was alive or dead or living-dead, *but he walked!* He carried the Colt and he had his boots on. I saw him!"

"It couldn't have been some one rigged up like him?"

"No, no! Majorie thought it was her father so completely," Quayne said, "that she is going to get an order to exhume his body tomorrow to make sure the corpse is still in its coffin."

"Some angle!" I said. "He was buried with that six-gun."

"And his boots."

"Did Norman go home too?" I asked.

"No," said Quayne. "He was too drunk. Boggs put him to bed. He slept through the whole thing. We had to carry him up. He doesn't know yet what happened."

"What was Lamont doing here?"

"The young ass is in love with Majorie—or she with him. I'm not sure. They're engaged, at any rate. I think he's a fortune-hunter. I wouldn't blame the old Major for walking in that case. But the ghost seemed to draw his gun on Ian, who was asleep."

"That's off the record—about Majorie," I said.

"Of course," said Quayne instantly.

Sergeant Hanley got to his feet and yawned. He was bored to death. He didn't have enough imagination to have a nightmare. You know, the kind of a guy who sees an ax murder and then has a hearty lunch.

"Somebody's kidding the hell outa you," he said. "We'll wait for further developments before we make a report at h.q. I've got to be going, Mr. Quayne. Don't take it too seriously."

"Thanks," Quayne said. "Hope you're right."

"I am," Hanley grinned. "Want a lift home, Daffy?"

"Them is kind words," I said, "and helps the ole swindle sheet along. 'Night, Quayne. Thanks for the yarn."

Hanley and I went down the steps to the drive and walked to the squad car which he had brought. "Poppa," I said as we neared it, "what you think, eh?"

"Nuts," Hanley said bluntly.

"Quayne—or the ghost?"

"Both." He sighed. "They're all kidding themselves."

"You don't believe the Major came back, then?"

"Daffy," he said gruffly. "I've been a cop for ten years. I never saw the stiff yet who could rise from the dead—and God knows I've handled enough of them. Aw, let's go home!"

He reached the car and put his hand on the doorknob to pull it open. He was on the driver's side across from me. He stopped and his eyes suddenly took on a stony glaze. I thought he was staring at me, but right away I could see that they were flicking over my right shoulder somewhere behind me. My own eyes fixed on his face. His lips tightened.

He croaked hoarsely; "God!"

I wheeled and followed the line of his gaze in dread. I don't know what I expected to see. Whatever it was—I didn't see it.

I gasped and felt an icy tingle shoot down my spine, studding my skin with goose-pimples and raising the hair on my neck straight out.

TO THE RIGHT of Quayne's castle, there was a row of tall shrubbery. Right close to the line of shrubbery something was walking towards us, with a peculiar lumbering gait.

For an instant it looked like a cloud. Then, as I focused it, more clearly, I saw that it was the ghost—the banshee in boots. Major Culpepper—whose corpse was somewhere in Woodlawn Cemetery—was walking right towards us across Quayne's shrubs. I could see the shrubs through him, waving from the river wind. He loped along, swinging that deadly grave-scratcher at his side.

He threw his head back and forth as though he were looking for some one. Then he straightened up and he glared at Hanley and me. He was hazy and gaseous and he looked like smoke. I could see his handle-bar mustache like Quayne had said. I couldn't open my mouth. I was frozen dumb with terror. The only feeling I had was the tickling of the sweat down my face even though the cold wind was hitting me there.

The ghost stopped walking and looked straight at us. Then it grinned. The Colt six-gun shot up without warning, and it fired at us. There was no sound. There was nothing but a billow of white smoke from the mouth of the barrel and a heavy pall of silence.

Something went by my ear, buzzing like a wasp. There was a tinkle behind me. I didn't have to turn. I knew a slug had broken through the windshield of the squad car. I croaked:

"Poppa!"

Hanley moved. He came around the front of the car with his service revolver in his hand and as he went by me, he fired twice at the ghost. The flame from his muzzle looked deep-orange in darkness.

The next things I knew, the ghost was gone into nowhere and Hanley was stomping around the shrubbery where it had been, his gun waving wildly in his paw.

The door of the castle squeaked open and Wilson Quayne shouted:

"My God! What's happened out there?"

Bill Hanley came back and put his gun away. He looked at Quayne and didn't know what to say. He was white as a sheet, and I was no help at all. I was sweating frost.

"What happened?" Quayne asked again. "I heard shots fired!"

"Naw," I gulped. "That was only this can back-firing."

"Y-yeah," Hanley said.

"But your engine isn't running!"

"It stalled," I said. "We got to see what was the matter with it. That's all. It stalled. Get in, Bill, and for God's sake, get the hell outa here!"

We reached Riverside Drive before we looked at one another and said anything. I broke the ice with:

"What—was it, Poppa?"

Hanley's paws were trembling. "Don't know, Daffy," he said.

"It shot at us."

"I know. Lookit that hole. A slug hit there, and it was a .32, if I'm a judge."

"Culpepper's Colt was a .31," I said.

"I—I know... A hundredth of an inch ain't much difference. That's a .31, really."

"Was it a spook, Poppa?"

"I never missed a target in my life," Hanley said. "My slug went right through it, Daffy. If it'd been alive—it'd be lying there now. But there wasn't anything!"

"Then you believe—"

Hanley grunted and hunched his shoulders. "I ain't saying. I ain't saying a thing any more tonight, Daffy. Forget it."

When we got downtown, it was only eleven-thirty and I had plenty of time to get to Dinah's but I didn't go. I went home and went to bed, but I had screwy dreams. So I got up and had a couple of Old-Fashions.

At three o'clock, being sufficiently oiled to sleep without dreams, I went home to bed again. I thought how damn silly the whole thing was. No crime. No one hurt. No hero, no villain, no heroine. All there was to write about was: *One ghost—when last seen, it was wearing boots and carrying a Colt six-shooter.*

It just didn't make sense.

3

THE TELEPHONE NEXT to my bed was jingling when I woke up. I reached over and picked up the receiver and said:

"Yeah?"

"Pardon me, Mr. Vanderastor," said the Old Man, "but did it ever occur to you that a newspaper known as the New York *Chronicle* pays you a salary each week to appear in its office around nine-thirty each morning and then make a pretense of working the rest of the day?"

"Hello, chief," I sighed. "What's wrong?"

"Wrong?" he echoed. "Nothing is wrong, my sluggard. I am only requesting that you report for work. It's eleven-thirty."

I looked at the clock. It was. "Holy, holy, chief," I said, "I'm sorry. I overslept. I didn't get to bed until—"

"Never mind that," said the Old Man. "Where's the ghost story? Every other rag in town has it but us."

"I didn't write it, chief," I said.

The Old Man is sharp. Instead of bawling me out, he muttered, "Then I was right. It's a bigger yarn than three sticks. That's all the space it got. What happened?"

"The ghost walked and I saw it."

"You saw it?" the Old Man yelled.

"Are you sure?"

"Hell's bells, chief, I never want to be that sure again. I dreamt about the damned thing all night. It shot at us and fired a live slug through Hanley's windshield!"

"Daffy," asked the Old Man gently, "are you sober?"

"Cold," I said.

"You saw a ghost? Not a man. Not a trick. A real ecto-plasmic ghost in boots and with a six-gun?"

"It was a genuine banshee," I said.

"We've got a yarn!" exclaimed the Old Man. "You know what's happened this morning? Majorie Culpepper got an exhumation order from the coroner's office. What does that mean?"

I jumped out of bed excitedly. "It means she's going to dig out the old man and see if he's gone zombi!"

"Get out to Woodlawn," snapped the Old Man. "Halloran told me she's due there at one. Cover that yarn. Break it in the Wall Street closing. And step on it!" He paused, "Got a camera?"

"I've got the Leica loaded," I said.

"Scram then. Get a hot shot."

I stepped on it. A little after one I was at Woodlawn, strolling towards a small cluster of people in front of a huge white mausoleum. I cut across the grass towards them and reached a uniformed flatfoot.

"Beat it," he said, waving his nightstick.

"Utsnay," I said, starting by.

He grabbed me by the shoulder and shoved me back.

"Hey," he said easily. "Maybe you didn't hear me. Beat it. This is private business."

"Listen, flatfoot," I bluffed, "maybe you don't know me. I'm Holmes of the bureau."

"Sure," he grinned, "and I'm Charlie Chan of the Honolulu police force. Scram, mister."

I sort of stared at him. He was the first guy I ever met who didn't fall for the Holmes gag. "But this isn't private, officer," I said. "Miss Culpepper took out exhumation papers. That's a public statement of intent to exhume a corpse."

"Don't tell me the law," he said. "Just beat it before I wrap this stick around your neck."

"Hey, Bill!" I yelled.

Sergeant Bill Hanley turned around from where he stood in front of the tomb and caught sight of me.

"Call off your dogs," I said.

"Let him through," said Hanley.

The cop flushed as I stuck out my tongue and murmured, "Holmes of the bureau, my man. Step aside." I went up to the tomb. There was Hanley, and Wilson Quayne and Van Lamont—I recognized him from pictures—all slicked up like a Greek god. And there was also the girl and another guy whom I'd never seen before.

The cemetery caretaker was fumbling at the keyhole of the doors of the tomb.

Van Lamont pushed his way towards me and snapped at Hanley, "Sergeant—who is this man?" His classic profile was slightly annoyed and his usual petulant expression was almost girlish.

"His name's Dill," said Hanley. "He's a reporter."

"A reporter?" Lamont exclaimed.

Majorie Culpepper looked me over at those words. She was a nice little brunette with bright blue eyes. She looked haggard. As though she'd been crying a lot.

I couldn't blame her. I had had the jitters all night myself from seeing that spook.

The man with her said, "But, Sergeant, a reporter! Good God, man, we're trying to keep this as quiet as possible. Don't you think—"

"Daffy's a good man," Hanley said. "Besides, he's in this as much as the rest of you. He's the guy who saw the thing with me last night out on Mr. Quayne's estate. He's holding the story back as long as possible."

"Maybe I won't break it at all," I said. "There's been no crime so far. I hope you noticed that the *Chronicle* was the only rag that didn't have a story on it this morning."

"Those asinine stories this morning!" Lamont sniffed.

Quayne looked at me. "Why did you lie to me last night?" he asked kindly. "You said the car back-fired."

"Two reasons,"I replied. "One—I wanted to get out of there in a helluva hurry. Two—I didn't want you to be scared the rest of the night." I nodded to the girl. "This is Majorie Culpepper, isn't it?"

"Yes," said Quayne. "And this is Mr. Ian Norman with her. You know Lamont?"

"I've seen him," I said dryly.

IAN NORMAN WAS about thirty-four. He was holding his black felt hat in his hand. His hair was thin at the crest of his temples. He was losing it. He wore tortoise-shell glasses.

"I've got it open," said the caretaker.

Norman put his arm around Majorie Culpepper. "I don't think you should go in, dear," he said softly. "After all, he's been—dead over six months."

"Ian's right," Quayne said. "It won't be pleasant."

Lamont sniffed and went to her side. He looked pale around the gills. "Don't worry, darling," he said in the voice Hollywood should have outlawed. "I'll stay here with you."

"Maybe you'd better," I said. We wouldn't want anyone getting sick in there."

The gal's eyes flicked on mine for a second as if in mutual understanding, then dropping quickly away to the ground as Lamont held her. I was puzzled. In the first place, I didn't see how anyone could fall in love with a Gila monster like Lamont, despite the fact that he had played the nuptial boards four times. Likewise he had established residence in Nevada four times. A much-married guy. Secondly, Majorie Culpepper looked like a swell kid to me, and not the kind of a gal who'd skid for such a ham.

Hanley had gone into the tomb. Then Quayne. Norman, nervous as the devil, waited for me. I smiled at him to cheer him up, because his hands were really trembling. He went in, and I followed him. Then came the caretaker.

Now, tombs aren't exactly hi-de-hey spots and this one was no exception to the rule. It was darkish inside, but through the glass panels of the door, you could see the smooth cold contour of the marble walls. It gave me a shivery feeling.

The caretaker unlocked the hinge on a marble slab and dropped it down. Quayne was sweating like a soda glass. Norman was white and violently trembling. I thought he was going to let go. Hanley was a little nervous about it. I knew how Norman felt. When I was a cub and saw my first corpse, I was the same way—with that sinking feeling in the pit of my belly.

I helped the caretaker when he reached in and pulled out

the coffin. It was a nice silver thing and it came out easily on rollers. It lifted right down to the portable stand the caretaker had brought without a bit of trouble. I was glad we didn't have any lifting to do. It looked heavy as lead.

The caretaker attacked the lid holders. I could hear Norman's breathing now, short and gaspy.

Finally the holders dropped down. It was a breathless sort of moment and I could feel the blood pounding through my head as I crowded in. I got the Leica out surreptitiously and held it in my right hand, sighting it by instinct between Hanley's and Quayne's shoulders. No one saw it. The caretaker lifted up the lid.

For a second or two, there wasn't a sound. Not even Norman's hoarse breathing.

Then I sighed and snapped the Leica.

I snapped it again to make sure. I turned and went out of the tomb. On the grass, Van Lamont and Majorie Culpepper stared at me stonily, their mouths open, their faces frankly asking a question.

"Sorry, Miss Culpepper. I've got to break the story," I said. "It's the first time in my life I've ever scooped the city press bureau on a metropolitan story and I can't let it go." I took a quick snap of her with Lamont and stuck the Leica in my pocket. Then I ran like hell down the lane towards the administration building by the storage vaults.

The ghost who wore boots, you see, had turned into live news, easily worth a two column twenty-four point head.

Major Culpepper's corpse, and his boots, and his Colt grave-scratcher, had vanished completely from his silver coffin.

4

BODY-SNATCHING STILL HAS that old ghoulish lure and when we broke that yarn we broke it proper. The Old Man laid it across the front page of the Wall Street closing edition and I even got there in time for a three column reproduction of the empty coffin, which cinched the yarn.

When it had come off the presses and I was admiring my by-line the Old Man called me in. I entered like Caesar returning to Rome.

"Daffy," he said, "that's a good story. It's going to shoot circulation tonight."

"It's not bad," I said, "but I had the breaks."

"For a follow-up," said the Old Man, "I'm going to use the ghost side of it more fully. You only insinuate in the story that the ghost Quayne and the others saw last night might have some connection. Now, you and I know it has got a good connection. Tomorrow I'm going to have you do a signed story, telling how you saw that ghost out at Quayne's estate, how you saw it was Major Culpepper and how it fired at you. It'll make a swell followup and the more weird you make it the better."

"Hell," I said, "I don't have to make it weird. It's the real McCoy. I'm just as interested in reading about it as the man on the street. The only thing is—I want more."

"That's the idea," said the Old Man. "Did you get a statement from Majorie Culpepper?"

"I was in too much of a rush," I answered.

"Well," he said, "run up and see her tonight. Not now. Every rag in New York is trying to see her now. Save it for tonight. And you might cheek the morgue and see if the corpse has turned up at all. Be thorough there. Any other ideas?"

"Yeah," I said. "I want the clippings on the gal and those on Quayne and Norman and Lamont too. There's something screwy there, chief. She's engaged to be married to Lamont, but she can't stand him. I could feel it. And Quayne seems worried as hell about something. And Norman is worried about Majorie. It's all as plain as day. I don't see what it has to do with the snatched corpse or the ghost, but it may tie in later."

"Good," said the Old Man. "Hit it. How do you suppose that stiff was snatched?"

"Easy," I said. "Master key to open the vault. Same for the crypt hinges. It can be done without much risk if you have a car waiting down on Webster Avenue. You yank out the stiff, shoot the coffin back, relock the door and throw the stiff over the railing. Then climb down and pick up the stiff again, shove him in the car and lam."

"Sounds simple."

"It was simple, I'll bet," I said.

"You don't suppose the corpse is being held for ransom?"

"No," I said. "No ransom there. That's my guess. It's gone because it's supposed to have risen from the dead and come back to haunt somebody."

"You don't know how long it's been out of the tomb?"

"Couldn't say. Not long, though. Just since somebody got this scatterbrained idea of the ghost."

"Okay, Daffy," the Old Man said.

"Hit the yarn."

I got the clippings on the four of them and pored through them. I found four interesting facts:

One: Majorie Culpepper had been engaged to marry Ian Norman in November, 1933, but broke it off after a trip to Los Angeles where she met Van Lamont.

Two: Quayne had a reciprocal contract with the Culpepper Munitions Company in the use of his steel for shells and firearms.

Three: Major Culpepper designated the control of his company to his daughter, Majorie, with Ian Norman as chief adviser and executor of the estate.

Four: Van Lamont had a smelly rep for marrying rich women, divorcing them with nice cash settlements, and looking for new victims. This last was on the queer. Lamont had some way of hooking women—and not all by his personal charm—if any.

I put on my hat and coat and hied away for the city morgue. In the outer office, I stopped by Dinah Mason's desk.

"Hello, my hollyhock," I said. "Sorry about last night. Did you hear it all?"

"Hello, ghoul," she returned. "I had inklings. What's all the chatter about ghosts?"

"On the level. I saw him myself. I wouldn't kid you, lady, but you nearly lost a close friend. The slug went by my left ear."

"No kidding," she said seriously, looking scared. "Daffy, are you all right?"

"Then you *are* nuts about me," I said. "When do we marry?"

"When you stop playing target and settle down to a nice steady job on the copy desk."

"But—"

"Move along, please," she said, smiling derisively. "You're blocking the aisle... Yes, madam? The advertising department is to your left."

I left the building marking an X down in my notebook for my fifty-fourth try at trapping her, and then took a cab down to the morgue. I made it in ten minutes. I don't like the morgue. It has a sort of deadish smell that gets into your lungs.

The place had a chill to keep the bodies from decomposing. It wasn't a nice chill. I made it short and sweet.

"I'm looking for an old one," I said.

"Sure, Daffy," said the guy in charge. Mike Claney was his name. "We got all kinds."

"This one I want, Mike, is pretty old. Six months at least."

"Say," Claney exclaimed mildly. He stopped and peered at me.

"What's the matter?" I asked.

"Nothing," he replied. "Just sorta queer. The police boat fished out a stiff last night." He grunted. "It was pretty old, too. Six months easily."

HE LED ME across the dull room to one of the cabinets. He reached up and yanked on the handle. The cabinet rolled out without a squeak. A still figure reposed on the slab with a white sheet over it. Claney threw the sheet back off the face.

I looked. It wasn't as bad as I thought. The flesh was yellow and stretched over the cheek bones as tight as a drum skin. The eyes were sunken, the mouth drawn down. On the upper lip, beneath each nostril, there were short clumps of hair, as though a mustache had been snipped off with a scissors.

"Found this way? Nothing else?" I said.

"He was found nude," said Claney. "Know who it is? We want to identify him."

"No," I lied. "He's not the one I want. Thanks, Claney."

"We got others—"

"No, no, never mind," I said. I went out and telephoned the Old Man. "I found him," I said.

"The major?"

"Yeah. At the morgue. Fished him outa the East River last night. He's probably been in since last night. Maybe the night before. Better break it tomorrow, It'll make a good streamer."

"Okay. You tell Majorie Culpepper on the q.t. and get a statement tonight."

"Right." I hung up. I called Ian Norman. "This is Daffy Dill," I said. "I want to see Miss Culpepper tonight when she's clear of reporters. Something important. Think you can arrange it?"

"You'll not bother her with questions?" Norman asked kindly. "She's quite upset, Dill. Really she is. The poor child's all awry."

"I found something," I said. "She ought to know."

"Very well," he said. "Come up to my place at about

eight. She'll be here. I'm having her stay here quietly. Until the fuss dies down. Please don't tell anyone else, on your honor."

"On my honor," I said sincerely.

"At eight, then."

5

NORMAN HAD THE penthouse on top of an apartment building on Park Avenue and Seventy-second Street. There was a private automatic elevator, too. I took it up, glancing at my watch as the hands pointed exactly to eight bells.

I was a little surprised when Inspector Halloran let me in. I didn't think that he'd be there. Bill Hanley was there, too. They both looked worried. Lamont and Majorie Culpepper were on the lounge. She looked even more haggard and Lamont was comforting her in a slithery way. He reminded me of an eel—only more so. Wilson Quayne was there. And the host, of course, Ian Norman; who looked very tired, despite his attempted cheerfulness for. Majorie's benefit.

I took a chair and sat down. I realized that everyone was staring at me.

"Hey—what is this?" I said.

"I told Inspector Halloran that you said you had found something vastly important," Norman said apologetically. "Sorry if I've ruined a scoop, but it's best that we work together on the thing, don't you think."

"Sure," I said. "I expected Halloran to hear it. But I didn't want it to get around or the morgue would be swamped."

Inspector Halloran said gruffly, "Daffy, you don't mean—"

I nodded. "Night before last. It's the Major, all right. But his gun and his boots were missing. And whoever snatched the body, clipped the handlebar mustache of his."

"Thank God for that, anyway," exclaimed Quayne sharply. "At least we can put him back in decent burial where he belongs. I'm—at sea as to the purpose behind all this...."

Norman sighed. "Purpose? I hadn't even gotten that far. I'm trying to figure out just what is happening!"

"I'll run along," said Inspector. Halloran, his big beefy face working, excitedly. "You too, Hanley. Thanks, Daffy. The morgue?"

"Claney'll show you the body. You can make official identification in the morning, and rebury."

"Yeah," Halloran nodded. Then he and Hanley went out the door.

Majorie Culpepper cried a little. But it was a relieved sort of crying. She felt better that we had located the body. Van Lamont kept patting her shoulder and saying, "Bear up, my darling. Be brave and strong." He sounded like a movie sub-title.

I was sitting uncomfortably there, squirming a trifle and waiting for the girl to get in shape enough to give me a statement on the recovery of the corpse, when it happened.

The room we were sitting in was about thirty feet long and twenty feet wide. A humdinger, with a fireplace at the far end. We were all just sitting there, perfectly peaceable.

Then every single light in that room blew out as though a fuse had been shorted. We were all sitting down, mind you, and I could see the main light plug across the room.

No one was near it, not a soul. But those lights went out just the same.

In the second that we were plunged into blackness, I couldn't see a damn thing. I felt my eyes popping as I stared and half rose from my chair.

It took about five seconds for my eyes to see again, even in the darkness. Up here on the penthouse, it was really black without lights. There were no other glimmers to reflect into the room. A violent tremor shook me as I heard the others begin murmuring.

And the ghost walked.

It was the Major—the dead and gone Major—looking towards us right out of the fireplace, the Colt six-gun in his right hand and the army boots on his legs. He looked to the right and the left. It was hard to distinguish his face, he looked so ghostly and hazy. He moved like rolling smoke, and this time his ectoplasmic stream dug into the floor not far from where I sat.

I was scared stiff. I couldn't move. I watched, transfixed, and waited. On the sofa, to my left, I dimly discerned Van Lamont leap to his feet and choke out a terrified ejaculation.

The ghost stopped looking right and left. It looked straight ahead. It grinned. The Colt six-gun flung up—just like it had at me on the Quayne estate the night before. The hammer went down and a white cloud of powder smoke billowed out of the barrel.

There was a ghastly thud. I had heard those kind before—a slug hitting flesh. Van Lamont groaned shrilly just once. I saw him fall. He hit the floor with a thump which rattled the prints on the wall. I stared at the ghost.

The Colt gun had dropped down and Major Culpepper was laughing heartily as though it were a huge joke. Suddenly, he faded from sight right where he stood. He just snapped into thin air.

MY VOICE RETURNED. I let out a wild yell and got up from my chair. I heard Majorie scream once, then nothing. Quayne lighted a match and went to the light switch. He clicked it a couple of times. The lights didn't work.

"Short circuit," he muttered. "Ian—call the house manager! Get a new fuse installed downstairs quickly!"

Norman moved past me to the phone. He called downstairs. I listened to him ask excitedly for the electrician. He explained that the lights had gone out. Then he asked the operator to get hold of Inspector Halloran at the morgue and tell him to come right out.

I spied a candle on a sidetable in the flicker of Quayne's match. I ran to it and grabbed it. I knocked a square little box to the floor. I struck a match of my own and lighted the candle. I put the box back on the table, noticing it was a roll of amateur panchromatic film, unused. I stared at it for a second. Then I took the candle and went over to the lounge.

I bent down. Van Lamont had fallen on his face. I turned him over. Quayne and Norman were at my side. The girl was out in a dead faint on the lounge.

There was a welt in the middle of Lamont's face, raised like a mosquito bite and flecked with a blue bubble. A slug had killed him instantly, gone through his brain. Yet there had been no sound. I was baffled. I knew you couldn't silence a pistol or revolver. The only thing you can put a silencer on is a rifle. And that makes a *plop*. This shot the ghost had fired didn't make even a *ping*.

Then somebody downstairs fixed the fuse and the lights were on again. We carried the girl into a bedroom before she could see what had happened. After that, we just waited, staring at one another's pale faces and wondering. I didn't even have the presence of mind to call the paper. I just wondered and kept wondering until Halloran arrived and found us there.

It was after midnight when we finally left. Questioning had gotten us nowhere. Each of us had seen the ghost. Each of us swore that he had seen the ghost shoot. Each of us swore we had heard no shot. It was an impasse. Halloran was stumped. Everyone was stumped. The Public Welfare boys arrived after the medical examiner and took Lamont away. The M.E. said it was a .32 slug, and that was all.

What a headline it was going to make!

GHOST KILLS ACTOR

And that was the way it would stand too! For Halloran couldn't shake the testimony, not even mine.

I left after they carted the corpse out. I went down the hall and then huddled up under a skylight near the roof and waited. After about half an hour, I saw Halloran and Hanley and Majorie Culpepper and Quayne leave the place and go down in the elevator.

I climbed down from the skylight and rang the doorbell. Ian Norman open it. He was surprised.

"I thought you'd gone," he said.

"I want to see you," I said.

I went in and he closed the door. I took a seat near the fireplace away from the bloody stain in the rug. He sat down opposite me, his face lined with weariness.

"Norman—let's lay our cards on the table," I said.

"I don't understand."

"I know you killed Lamont," I said evenly.

"You're insane," Norman cried.

"I know how you made the ghost, too," I said.

He shot his hand into his shirt and whipped it out. I stepped forward out of my chair and clipped him neatly on the chin, not too hard. It knocked him over backwards in the chair and sent him sprawling on his skull. Then I dove on him, caught his right hand and took the gun he had in it away from him. I looked at it.

"Thought so," I said. "Pneumatic pistol. No wonder it didn't make any noise."

Norman sat up on the floor and stared at me. There was a reddish welt on his chin and he rubbed it painfully.

"You damned fool—what did you do that for?" I said.

"You said—"

"I know what I said. But if you kill me, you'll fry sure! You couldn't get away with that, not after Lamont."

Norman sighed and set the chair up again. He sat down in it heavily. "All right, Dill," he said. "You've caught me. But I don't care. I've done a good job killing that rat, a good job."

"Agreed," I said. "If ever a man deserved killing, it was Van Lamont. But you certainly made preparations. Let's take it slow. When did you plan first to get him?"

"A month ago," said Norman dully.

"Don't talk like the noose is around your neck," I said.

"I'm an all-right guy. I like that kid, Majorie, as much as you do. I'm no cop. I don't have to turn you in."

"You mean—"

"Talk," I said. "That's all now. Just talk."

"SHE TOLD ME a month ago," Norman said. "She was frantic then, because she hated him so. She didn't want to marry him. She thought I might be able to help her...."

"The rat had something on her," I said. "He was blackmailing her into marriage?"

"Yes."

"What was it?"

"She wrote some indiscreet letters. He framed her, and then he threatened her with a breach of promise suit and what not if she didn't marry him. He said he'd rake the whole dirty mess into a court room. She couldn't do a thing. She hated him then, of course."

"So?"

"When she told me a month ago, I was stuck. I didn't know what to do. I'd have liked to have killed him, but I didn't want the chair for a good deed."

"Go on."

"One night shortly after she told me, I ran off a couple of my old reels of film for myself. I'm an amateur moviemaker you know. I had this one of Major Culpepper. I remember when we made it. He was supposed to stalk prey, look right and left, and finally sight at the camera and fire.

"As I watched it and thought of how he would have felt if he had known of Lamont's trickery. I was struck with an idea. If Major Culpepper could come back from the dead and kill Lamont—no living man could possibly be executed for the crime, not even myself. So I went to work.

I blacked out the background on the film, leaving just the figure of the major. Then I threw him slightly out of focus and gave him that gaseous, hazy look."

I shivered. "It sure was realistic." I pointed to his leg. "And you got a small projector—one of those special palm-size models—and strapped it on your leg, running the light with batteries on your person, right?"

Norman nodded. "Then it was easy for me to lift my trouser leg, turn on the projector by a simple switch in my lapel and turn it off likewise. Then I had to add realism—to make it look as though the major had really returned. If I could make it good enough—and get a man like Quayne to certify the ghost's existence, it was sold!"

"So you snatched the corpse," I said. "And stripped it and dumped it in the East River. What did you do with the boots and Colt?"

"Dumped them into the river, too. That was the night before we went to Quayne's. It was a simple job. After that, I had to establish the ghost. I acted tight at Quayne's, and while lying on the sofa while the lights were down, I shot the vision of the hazy Major on the tapestry opposite."

"It worked, too," I said. "But why in hell did you try to kill me out on the grounds when Hanley and I were leaving?"

"I was careful *not* to kill you," Norman said. "I shot at the car, just to make it credible that a ghost could fling bullets. I shot from my window. I had leveled the projector against the shrubbery from there, too."

"Why, though?"

"You were a reporter—to give the ghost the publicity

and make it real. Hanley was a policeman—to make the police think there actually was a ghost that could kill."

"I see," I said. "After that, it was just a matter of letting the ghost kill Lamont."

"Yes," he said dully. "As it was, they couldn't get me. Then you found me out."

"Yeah," I said. "I found you out. Norman—you overlooked one thing in killing Lamont."

"What was that?"

"The evidence he has against Majorie. Where are those letters?"

Norman smiled craftily. "They were in his apartment. I got them. I burned them. That side is all clear."

I nodded. "Give me that projector."

He pulled up his trouser leg and unstrapped the machine. It was a small, compact little thing, only about four inches long, built to take only about twenty feet of sixteen millimeter film. I stripped off the film and tossed it on the fire. It burned like a flash. I stuck the projector in my pocket with the pneumatic pistol. I got up.

"FORGET IT," I said. "Your story is—like mine and the others—that the ghost who wore boots killed Van Lamont."

"Wh-what are you going to—do with those?" he asked hoarsely.

"Dump them off George Washington Bridge," I said.

"Oh, thank God," he said and broke down in a series of quiet sobs. I never saw a man look so tired.

"One more thing," I said. "How'd you work the short circuit?"

"I had two wires from the lamp under the rug, raised

above each other and scraped bare. I stepped on them and blew the fuse. Their own tensile recoil pulled them apart for the next installed fuse to work without my touching them.

"Smart," I said. "Fix it right tonight so there'll be no comeback when Halloran goes over this place tomorrow."

"I will," he said. "Why—why are you doing this?,"

"Majorie's a good kid. And I like you."

"But—can I be sure—"

"I'll say you can! Listen, Norman, when my paper says a ghost killed Lamont instead of an ordinary man, the circulation will rocket. Just another reason for dumping these things in the Hudson."

"But how—can I be sure—?"

"Mister," I grinned, "if they get you, they can get me too as an accomplice after the fact. Aiding a homicide and all that." I waved good night.

When I did drop those things off the bridge next day, I thought how crazy the whole thing was and how it never possibly could have happened.

But it did—just the same!

THE EGG

One of those stories you read and remember because—It's one of those stories!

1

I HADN'T GOT ten feet inside of the Hideaway Club when a hand pounded the back of my right shoulder and Bill Latham, the proprietor, exclaimed: "Daffy Dill! Where in hell have you been?"

I said "Hello, my fran!" and grinned weakly.

He took me by the arm and steered me straight to the bar where "Shorty" McGinnis, as red-faced as ever, was tossing the giggle-water to and fro for the paying customers.

"Anything Daffy wants," Latham said, "is on the house, Shorty."

"Holy, holy!" I said. "Are you feeling good? Who hopped you up?"

Latham grinned and lighted a cigar. "Nix, Daffy. I like you; that's all. Hell, you ain't been in to see me since that night you oiled yourself up after you said you'd seen a ghost."

"Yeah." I nodded. "I remember that."

"You ought to come in more often," Latham said. "Only night before last, two society dames were in their cups and started to pull each other's hair. It would have made a sweet little yarn if you'd heard some of the nice things they said about each other. Whooey! You couldn't have printed it verbatim. The Old Man would never have stuck it in the *Chronicle's* columns. By the way—how is he?"

"Still nuts," I said. "An old-fashioned, Shorty."

"I get it," said Latham. "He's making you cover a screwy story. You're on the prowl, ain't you?"

"Yeah," I said; "and I feel like a flatfoot. The Old Man don't care two pins for my young life."

Latham looked interested. "It couldn't be an—interview with Joey Keel?"

"Bull's-eye," I said. "Give the man a cigar, Shorty."

"Umm," Latham muttered. "Keel's here, you know, Daffy."

"Do I know? I tailed him here. I've been tailing him all night trying to get up my nerve to see him."

"Scared?"

"Sort of," I said. "Not so much of Keel. More of those two kill-crazy mugs of his. You know, Frankie Barber and the Canteen. I looked cross-eyed at the Canteen once and he nearly shot me on suspicion."

I drank my old-fashioned slowly as Bill Latham smiled and said:

"Keel's alone, Daffy. He's a human guy. Go on up and see him. And you'd better do it before Barber and the Canteen get here. He's expecting them, you know."

I finished my drink and set down the glass. "O.K."

"It's the four-hundred-grand-armored-car heist, ain't it?" Latham asked.

I nodded. "Keel's out on bail. He's got an alibi and he's clean with the law, but the Old Man wants me to see if I can't get something, anyway."

"What the hell!" Latham shrugged. "Keel ain't a bad egg.

A little hard-boiled but otherwise on the up. Go ahead and see him."

I sighed. "O.K., Nemesis," I said. "But if the department of street cleaning finds my handsome young corpse littering somebody's nice clean sidewalk to-morrow morning, you can hold yourself morally responsible for the burial, Bill."

"O.K. by me!" Latham laughed. "But if it bothers you so much, why don't you fake the yarn or tell the Old Man that Keel wouldn't say anything for publication?"

"Ah," I groaned, "it's the newsy nose and Abyssinian blood in me. I'm always sticking my peninsula into other men's businesses. I'll see him, heigh-ho! Where is he?"

"Upstairs in room 3."

I SHOOK LATHAM'S hand solemnly and then strode away from the bar. I cut back through the Hideaway to the rear of the spot and then went up the narrow stairs there to the private party rooms that Latham kept up for incognito brawls of the rich.

There were four private rooms up on the balcony, each with a number on the door. With nervous fingers, I lighted a cigarette and then walked over to No. 3. I took a deep breath and then rapped on the door a couple of times.

There was a long wait and nothing happened.

Just as I raised my paw to pound again, I heard Joey Keel's voice rap out:

"Come in!"

I opened the door and stepped in. Keel was sitting behind a table directly across from me. He was the smallest killer I had ever seen, a little man no taller than five feet. He had a lean wolfish face and black hair. He was smoking and, as I looked at him, he exhaled a blue cloud of smoke which nearly hid the pistol he had on me. Then I saw it in his hand. "For cripes' sake!" I exclaimed. "Put that damn cannon away! I've got a weak heart."

He stared at me for a few seconds without moving. His thin lips broke into an amused smile as he watched my face. He threw up the muzzle of the pistol and jammed it back into its holster on the left side of his chest under his coat.

"Have a seat," he said softly, out of the side of his mouth, and his lips didn't even move.

I fell into a chair thankfully and began to breathe again.

He fixed his little gray eyes on mine and seemed to bore into me as he said: "You're Daffy Dill of the *Chronicle*, ain't you?"

"Yowzah," I said.

"Spill it, then," Keel said tersely. "You picked me up when I left my spot on West 10th Street. You tailed me to the Casino de Paree and waited until I came out. Then you followed me to the Hideaway."

"Holy smoke!" I said. "I thought that—"

"Sure, sure!" he said quietly. "You thought you were being fast. You were tailing the great Keel and he didn't know it. Well, Dill, he did know it. And he doesn't mind telling you that you nearly got cooked once. What's the lay?"

"Th-the lay?" I faltered.

"Sure!" he said. "Did the D.A. put you on me? Is he afraid to use his own flatfeet for bull business? Afraid I'm gonna jump bail?"

I held up my hand. "Wait a second, Keel," I said. "I'm a reporter, not a cop. Don't get me mixed up like that."

"Then what's the lay?"

"Well," I said, breathing deep, "the Old Man—"

"Who?" he snapped.

"My city editor," I replied, "got a brainstorm this afternoon after you'd posted your bond on that heist rap. He wanted an interview with Joey Keel. Me being the only available sucker in the office—he told me to cover."

Keel scowled and his eyes flashed. "Why all the hocus-pocus, then? Why didn't you interview me?"

I grinned weakly and put out my cigarette. "I was sorta—scared."

"Scared? Of me?" Keel began to look human. A smile curled the corners of his mouth and then broke into a light laugh. "That's hot," he said. There was a twinkle in his eyes.

"Why, Dill, why should you be scared of Joey Keel? I'm just a respectable, law-abiding citizen."

"That's what you say," I replied. "But I've been to the morgue, mister, and the air there is awful bad for a healthy young fellow."

"O.K., Dill," Keel said amusedly. "What do you want to know? I suppose your editor told you to ask me if I'd really done that four-hundred-grand job?"

"Yeah," I said. "Did you?"

"I am innocent," he replied, chuckling. "Innocent as a lamb. I want the public to know that. I want them to know that the D.A. is just trying to frame me for every job pulled off in this fair city."

"O.K.," I said. "But off the record, Keel, how do things look? The D.A.'s made his arrest. Will it stand?"

"Off the record," Keel said, "and I mean *off*, Dill—understand?"

"Yeah."

"The D.A. is whistling in the dark. He won't even get an indictment on me, much less a trial. I've got a foolproof alibi for the time of that heist."

"How about Barber and the Canteen?"

Keel grinned. "They were with me."

"But look," I said, "the driver of the armored car says he recognized the voice of the guy who stuck the tommy gun in his ribs as yours."

Keel looked mildly amazed. "My, my," he said, "but he must be mistaken! In the first place, the bandits were masked, weren't they?"

"You should know," I said boldly.

"Then how will his testimony stand up? The voice of a

masked man against an iron alibi. Dill, the grand jury will throw him out. You can't bring in an indictment on that."

"But maybe—" I started to say.

THERE WAS A knock on the door that cut me off. It was hollow and sharp and I skidded for the opposite side of the room like a cake of ice. Keel regarded me curiously as he lifted out his pistol again and held it on the door.

He asked: "What in hell's biting you?"

"I heard," I said, "you were expecting Barber and the Canteen."

Keel laughed. "You're off your nut," he said. "I've got a date with a doll here. Barber and the Canteen ain't coming."

The knock rapped out again.

Keel called in a low voice: "Open it and come in."

The door opened. A man stood there. Before Keel could see who it was, he clipped: "Hands away from your sides, mister."

The man exclaimed: "Joey! What the hell—"

Keel got to his feet and put the gun away, staring hard at the stranger. He was a tall, thin palooka with a thick black mustache on his upper lip. He had on a black derby and a cigar was tilted up in the left corner of his mouth. From portraits in the rogue's gallery, I recognized him as Frankie Barber, Keel's right-hand man.

Keel said coldly: "Step in, Frankie. Close the door."

Barber came across the sill, eyed me peculiarly, and then shut the door after him. He started to put his hands in his pockets, but Keel's eyes narrowed and he slowly shook his head. Barber seemed surprised, Keel suspicious.

"Well, Frankie?" Keel asked.

Barber glanced at me and snapped "Lam!" out of the side of his mouth.

I aimed for the door.

"Wait a sec, Dill," said Keel. "You're staying. I don't get this play at all."

"Listen," I said plaintively, "I've got to see a man about—"

Keel motioned to a chair. "Squat, Dill."

I squatted.

"Now, Frankie," Keel said, "how come?"

"How come what?" Barber exclaimed. "I don't get you, Joey! I had a date here with—"

He paused.

"Who?" Keel asked.

"Rose Fanta," Barber replied reluctantly.

"Rose Fanta!" Keel snapped. "Is that straight, Frankie? Don't give me the runaround!"

"On the level, boss," Barber answered quickly. "She called me up around six and said for me to meet her in No. 3 at the Hideaway at ten thirty to-night."

"The dirty little rat!" Keel growled ominously. "She called me at six and gave me the same line."

"She did?"

"Yeah." Keel stroked his chin and his face tightened. "What's it mean, Frankie?"

"I dunno," Barber replied hoarsely. "Hones', chief, I thought she was giving me a play!"

"You and me both," Keel said.

I asked: "Who's Rose Fanta?"

"Just a dame," Keel answered, staring at me again. "Just a dame you won't write about, Dill." He turned to Barber.

"This is a plant, Frankie. She got us out of the way here to work something else."

"But who—" Barber began.

"I got an idea," Keel said. He started for the door. "Come on. You, too, Dill."

"Me?" I said. "Hell, Keel, I'm not in on this! I got my interview. That's all I want."

"You're coming along," Keel said evenly. "If you're a good boy who's kept his nose clean, you'll be O.K. But if you put Rose Fanta up to calling us so the D.A. could search my place—"

"Whoa!" I cried. "I'm clean! I don't know Rosa Fanta!"

"I never saw a newspaperman yet who told the truth," Keel said. "You come along or Frankie'll dust one off your nose."

I sighed: "No violence, no violence, gentlemen. My weak heart, you know. I'm coming."

2

THE THREE OF us went out of the door and climbed down the stairs. Barber stayed ahead of me, Keel behind me, and I felt like a corpse riding in a hearse between two coffin lids. I was sweating and freezing at the same time.

I waved good night to Bill Latham as we passed him and he looked pleased as hell. He must have thought that I was making a big hit with Keel to be leaving with him.

Meanwhile, I had visions of all the newspaper headlines I'd written for "taken-for-a-ride" victims and I could see my own obit in neat black type on the first page of the second section.

We reached the street. We stood all bunched together for a second or so.

Keel asked: "Did you bring your car, Frankie?"

"No," Barber replied.

"I'll get a cab," Keel said.

He moved away from us toward the curb. He stood there for a few seconds, waiting for a hopeful hack to cruise by so that he could hail it.

None came.

Barber nudged me and said "Come on, Dill," and started toward Keel on the curbing.

I followed reluctantly. Out of the corner of my eye, down the block a little way, I saw a girl hop into a black sedan. I just had a flashing glimpse of her—a red coat, no hat, dark hair, and then, as I turned, the door of the sedan closed. Keel was still searching the street for a hack. I watched the black car. It went into gear, its motor purring. A twist of the wheels and the driver shot it away from the curb.

As it cleared the line of parked cars, I gasped. The girl in the red coat was driving herself. A sort of premonition hit me. The curtains in the back of the car were down, hiding the whole interior. The girl stepped on the gas, and the black car moved up the street toward the canopy of the Hideaway.

I went white as I saw the barrels of a shotgun sneak over the edge of one of the windows in the back of the car. The muzzles looked like the ends of fourteen-inch guns to me. With a wild yell to Keel and Barber, I dived aside in a beautiful jackknife and landed dexterously behind the protection of the front wheels of a parked car.

Keel and Barber looked at me as though I had gone crazy.

The next instant, thunder roared. Barber's head lopped back over his shoulders, nearly torn in half, as gore poured down over his coat. His derby hit the sidewalk and rolled into the revolving doors of the Hideaway. I remember that as plain as day.

Before his body could hit the ground, thunder roared again. This time I could see the flashing fire of the shotgun followed by a huge billow of smoke.

Keel screamed once as the charge hit him. He spun around from the blow twice—like a top—before he lost his balance and toppled over flat on his back.

A police whistle was shrilly shrieking as the black sedan

spurted away. I couldn't get the license number. The tail light was out. I got to my feet. My knees were stinging from the bruises I got in landing on them. I stumbled over to Barber.

He was lying on his face. There wasn't any of his neck left, just a raw gaping hole that looked horrible. He was dead as hell. I stepped over him to Joey Keel as Bill Latham came through the revolving doors, saw the mess, and cried:

"By cripes, Daffy!"

"Hijack," I gasped. "Black car with a sawed-off shotgun. I saw it and ducked. Barber's dead."

Latham blanched. "So's Keel."

Keel turned over on his good side at that instant and groaned. I went to him and lifted his head. Both his hands were tugging at his left side. They were covered with blood and there wasn't much of his side left whole. A buckshot charge at that distance is no bird gravel. Nine out of ten die without groaning.

"The rat!" Keel breathed. "The—yellow—rat—"

"Take it easy, Keel," I said. I cradled his head in my arm and yelled to Latham: "Get a cab, Bill!"

A crowd started to gather. A cop elbowed his way through and took charge.

Keel kept whispering. "The—rat—"

People were oh-ing and aw-ing all over the place. Suddenly a horn blew and brakes squealed as a hack drove in to the curb.

I got up with Keel in my arms. He hardly weighed anything at all, he was so small.

The cop grabbed my arm. "Where you going with 'im?" he bellowed.

"You damn fool!" I snapped. "He's alive! I'm heading for a hospital. Bill!" I called Latham. "Explain to this guy!"

"I will," Latham said. "Let him go, McGuire! What hospital, Daffy?"

"Bellevue," I said. I put Keel on the seat and climbed in beside him. I turned to the driver. "Did you hear that? Bellevue Hospital, mister, and drive like hell!"

GEARS GROUND, THE engine whined furiously, and we shot away from the curb with a jerk that tossed me back on the seat with a reverberating thump. Keel groaned and writhed in agony. He was bleeding like a broken dam and the cab was a mess.

"Hurt bad?" I asked, patting him.

He had what it takes. He looked up at me and a ghost of a smile flitted across his lips. "N-naw," he whispered. "It's—just—a—scratch."

"A sawbones'll fix you up in a few minutes," I said. "We're on the way to Bellevue."

He shook his head and groaned again, stiffening a little. "No go," he said. "No—sawbones. Undertaker—gets the job."

"Nuts!" I said. "You'll come through this."

He whispered: "Dill—"

I could hardly hear him. He was sinking down on the seat slowly. I said: "Yeah, Keel?"

"Thanks," he said faintly. He shuddered.

For a second, I thought he had gone and I pounded the driver on the back and told him to step on it.

Then Keel said: "In my pocket—Dill—"

"Take it easy," I cautioned.

"Got—to tell you," he said "In my pocket—an egg—"

"Yeah?"

"You—keep it," he whispered.

"Listen," I said. "Hang on, Keel. We're nearly there now! Can you hear me? Hang on!"

"No—use—"

"Keel!" My voice was sharp. "Who did it? Did you see who it was? Who shot you?"

He shook his head vaguely and his eyes closed. His last words were barely audible and I had to bend down and strain to catch them.

"Keep—egg—the one—who asks you—for it—"

"The one who asks me for it did it?" I asked quickly.

He sighed and murmured "That's—got it," and then his head fell down on his chest and his hands dropped away from the hole in his side for the first time.

I stared at him for a long moment. In repugnance, I reached around to the right side of him and felt in his coat pocket. There was the egg. I thought how damn lucky it was that the charge had hit his left side instead of his right. Vice versa and that egg would have been neatly scrambled a la buckshot.

I slipped the egg in my own pocket. I leaned forward then and tapped the driver on the shoulder.

"Yeah, boss?" he asked excitedly.

"Take it easy," I said. "Never mind Bellevue now."

He asked: "Where to?"

"The morgue," I replied dully.

3

IT WAS ELEVEN thirty when I dragged my tail into my own apartment. I was tired—not so much from the ruckus at Centre Street after Keel's body was tabulated in the morgue, but more from the sheer nervous tension of seeing two men die.

I'd played pretty square with Inspector Halloran at h.q. I'd told him all I knew about the shooting. But I neglected to mention Rose Fanta, nor did I mention the egg in my pocket and the last words Keel had spoken.

I knew I had a story for the *Chronicle* here somewhere and naturally I saved it.

I hadn't been home ten minutes when the "Old Man" called.

"Daffy, my angel," he squealed. "Give me the low-down!"

"Nothing doing, chief," I said. "You're running an afternoon paper and you'll have your story for the home edition to-morrow and not before. Judas, mister, Lincoln freed the slaves in '65!"

"All right, all right," he said and hung up in a huff.

I sat down at my desk and took the egg out of my pocket. It was an ordinary egg, brownish-skinned. I tapped it on the desk and it had a heavy sound. Holding it up to the electric light, I found I couldn't see the yolk. It was hard-boiled.

So I went over the shell minutely, even holding a five-and-dime magnifying glass on it to see if there was any writing anywhere. There wasn't, and I felt disappointed. The next thing that occurred to me was that the famous Rajah Whosis's ruby might be inside. That came from reading thrillers at night.

I broke the shell and peeled it carefully off. I was disappointed again. The white of a hard-boiled egg—as natural as ever—came through as I tossed the discarded pieces of shell into a wastebasket. Baffled, I stared at the egg and then revolved it slowly in my hand.

I stopped and sucked, in my breath so that it sounded like the 5:15 at a grade crossing.

There was writing on the white of the egg.

I picked up the magnifying glass feverishly and played it over the writing. The hand was a fine script, apparently very carefully written and the words themselves were a dark brown against the stark white albumen.

I read: "John Delano—Box 212—National Bank & Trust."

That was all, but it was pretty neatly done, and somehow it seemed familiar. I thought on it for a while, and suddenly it dawned on me where I'd read this sort of thing before. I got up and went to my bookcase and took out Richard Rowan's "Spies and the Next War." I didn't have any trouble finding the paragraph I wanted. It said:

> Hard-boiled eggs recently were found to be used by Soviet agents as a means of sending secret messages. These eggs were placed with fresh eggs going ostensibly to market. When the shells of the hard-boiled eggs were broken, it was found that

> the solid "white" had on its surface a distinct dark-brown lettering. Investigation revealed that a solution of sugar and alum makes a writing fluid which leaves no visible trace on the shell of the boiled egg, but leaves a very clear impression on the solid albumen inside—

So much for how it was done. I put the book away. Now why? And what did the terse words signify?

Later it all seemed perfectly simple, but right then I was thick enough not to see the solution. So I looked up the name "Rose Fanta" in the telephone book. I found it listed with an address in the Village, on Charles Street.

I said "Hi-ho, what've I got to lose?" and put on my hat and coat and hiked over to Fifth Avenue.

I was late and busses were as scarce as gold-backed notes. I stepped into a cab by the curb.

"Where to, Mac?" the driver asked.

"The Lost Generation," I replied.

"What?"

"Charles Street in the Village, ignoramus. I'm surprised at you!"

He grinned. "Sure, sure," he said as though he was humoring a lunatic and then drove down Fifth.

THE HIDE-OUT ON Charles Street was one of those antique little houses with flower boxes painted green and looking bare, hanging underneath a couple of crooked windows. The panes were so crooked I didn't see how the glass stood it without breaking.

I looked at the doorbell, found her name as plain as day, and gave her a buzz. The ticker answered, and I stepped in. The stairs were crooked, too, worse than the windows.

I wondered whether she lived on the first or second floor, but just then the door to the first-floor apartment opened and a blonde looked out and called:

"Yes?"

I said: "Rose Fanta?"

"That's my handle, mister," she said. "Is it magazines, books, or vacuum cleaners?"

"At this time of night?" I said. "My, my!"

"What's your racket?" she asked suspiciously.

"Tabbing corpses," I answered. "My name's Holmes. Homicide bureau. I want to ask you a couple of questions."

"Holmes?" she echoed. "I don't know any—" She caught herself and then said: "Step inside, copper."

"Don't mind if I do," I said, and I stepped in.

She had a nice little dive there, furnished with modern fire-sale tables and chairs and minus the red velvet trimmings which most molls and floozies like her go in for. The room was brightly lighted, and I could see her much better than in the hall.

I looked her over carefully. My blood sort of spurted as I noticed the resemblance she bore to the gal who had driven the murder car past the Hideaway. The same deep-set eyes and pointed chin. She was good-looking, not pretty or anything, but there was a come-hither quality in her face which must've hit the boys hard. Her hair was a deep yellowish blond, and right there I was thrown out at home.

The gal in the murder car had black hair. That was one thing I had seen, and it was probably the one thing some one else had seen in the mad rush of things. Black hair and a red coat.

"Sit down," she said, pointing to a chair.

I grabbed a seat and lighted a cigarette, noticing at the same time that there was another room somewhere beyond the end of this one, but that it was hidden from me by a pair of drapes. I began to feel cold. Those drapes moved a little, as though somebody was standing behind them and taking in every word. But it was too late to back down on the bluff then.

"Know Joey Keel, Rose?" I asked.

"Sure!" she answered easily. "Joey's a good friend of mine."

"And Frankie Barber?"

"Sure!"

"Friends of yours, eh?"

She nodded and her red mouth hardened. "Why not?"

I shrugged. "I dunno. I kind of thought if they were friends of yours, you'd have kept the date you made with each one of them in room No. 3 at the Hideaway for ten thirty to-night."

That got her. She twitched as though something had stung her and color came up into her cheeks.

She said: "You're blowing off, copper. I didn't have a date with them to-night."

"Baby," I said, "there's no hayseed in my hair. I know you did. I was with Keel and Barber while they were waiting for you."

"I didn't have no date with 'em," she repeated.

"Keel said you did. Barber said you did."

"You'll have a hot time proving that," she said, "with both of 'em dead."

"Well, well," I said, getting up. "You're quick on the draw, ain't you, Rose? How'd you know they were dead?"

Rose Fanta trembled momentarily, then steadied herself. "I—heard it on the radio. Short-wave police calls."

"Not on that radio," I pointed. "That's no short-wave set. Now come clean, sister! You saw them bumped! You saw them bumped from the front wheel of the car that had the guy who killed them!"

"I didn't!" she cried angrily.

"Have you got a red coat?" I asked.

"No."

"Let me feel your hair."

"Keep your dirty paws off me. This hair of mine is dry. It's been blond for the last four months and I've got witnesses for that."

"Then cart out the black wig you wore," I snapped.

The color left her cheeks and she glanced at the drapes. "You know a lot, don't you?" she said softly.

"There's one thing," I said, "that I don't know. Who was in the back of that car?"

"I don't know anything about it," she said.

"Don't lie!" I exclaimed harshly. "Who was in the back? Who handled the sawed-off shotgun?"

"I DID," SAID a new voice.

And it turned me into ice. I came around slowly and faced the drapes. A squat man with the broadest shoulders outside of Carnera, stood there, smiling a dead smile at me, his eyes as expressionless as a fish's. In his right hand—a hairy paw with short thick fingers—he held an automatic with which he covered me. I took a deep breath and said: "The Canteen!"

"It's about time," Rose Fanta snapped to him. "He was getting ready to book me!"

"Book you?" said the "Canteen." "Don't be a sap all your life, Rosie. This mug couldn't book you if he tried."

His voice was oily with smoothness and it didn't have any tone.

Rose Fanta asked: "How come?"

"Because," the Canteen replied without effort, "that Holmes of the homicide bureau is just a gag of his."

"You mean he ain't a copper?" she asked shrilly, throwing me a look that even a beauty soap wouldn't have cleansed.

"He's a reporter," replied the Canteen. "His name's Dill, and he worked on the *Chronicle.*"

"Works," I said.

"No," he returned, smiling, "worked. You're quitting your job to-night, Daffy. By accident."

He gestured with the gun and Rose Fanta thought he was going to give it to me right then.

She yelled: "Not here, you fool! They'll hear the shot—"

"Shut up!" he said coolly. "You talk too loud and too much. Get your coat on. I know just the ditch for this guy."

My mind was swimming as he came across behind me and jammed the gun muzzle against my ribs.

"Walk easy," he said. "Get in the black car. Any monkey biz and out goes the light."

I clutched at a straw as he moved me toward the door. Shrugging, I said: "O.K., Canteen. It's your party." I paused. "Still—"

He stopped at the door suddenly and relaxed the gun on my side. "Still what?" he asked eagerly.

I didn't say anything. Rose Fanta came into the room. But her hair wasn't blond any more. Her hair was black.

She had the wig on and she leered at me: "Good guess, Dill. Too good."

She had on a black coat this time, too. And under her left arm, she carried the red one all bundled up.

"Why'd you bring that?" the Canteen asked evenly.

"It's hot," Rose replied. "I'm not leaving it around here, Canteen. I'm dumping it over his body when you give it to him. They can't trace it. There's not a mark left in it. And I'm gonna burn this damn wig the minute we get back. Let's go."

The Canteen didn't make the slightest move toward the door. He stared at me and I managed an insolent smile as though bumping me wouldn't do a bit of good at all. He expected that smile, too. His fishy eyes took on some intelligence and he frowned.

"You were saying, Dill?"

"Who—me?" I feigned.

"Yeah."

I shrugged again. "I was thinking," I said, "you must feel pretty empty to knock off Barber and Keen and then not get what you bumped them off for."

"Meaning?" the Canteen purred.

"The four hundred grand the three of you heisted."

"Say!" Rose Fanta exclaimed. "He's a bright boy!"

"So you know that, too," the Canteen said. "You know Keel and Barber and me heisted the truck. Then you know that Rosie drove the car. And you know that I bumped Barber and Keel and didn't find the four hundred grand where Keel put it after the heist."

I warned. I knew I wasn't due to die now and I began to get the whole set-up. Keel had evidently planted the hot money after the holdup in a spot the three of them knew. Afraid of a double cross, Keel had apparently switched the four hundred grand to a new hideout. The Canteen had evidently felt the old itch to squander all of the haul without a three-way split. He had bumped Keel and Barber, and then gone to the cache for the dough. But it hadn't been there.

"Dill," asked the Canteen, "were you the third guy with them when they went down? The guy who jumped behind that car?"

"Check," I said.

"Did—Keel die right off?"

"He lived," I said, "for about ten minutes."

"Did he talk?"

I nodded grimly. "He talked. He didn't squeal, but he talked."

The Canteen smiled a dead smile again and I shuddered at the sight of it. His lips puffed out and his eyes looked eager. "Did he give you an egg?" he asked softly. "A hard-boiled egg?"

LIKE COLD WATER striking my face, Joey Keel's last words rushed back into my mind: The one—who asks you—for it—

"Why an egg?" I asked.

The Canteen's eyes glittered. "Still thinking of your story for the *Chronicle,* ain't you?"

"I just asked."

"Well, I'll tell you. Joey double crossed me. He double-crossed Barber, too, but Barber'll never know it. We cached that haul. And when I pulled into the cache to-night after the bump, the cash was gone."

I asked casually: "Where was the cache?"

"That's something," the Canteen replied, smiling, "you'll never know. I'll have occasion to use it again About the egg—it might amuse you. When I was in hiding upstate two years ago after George Billings was knocked off, the only way Joey Keel could get word to me without giving my hide-out away was by sending me food under an assumed name. Through the mails, see? He read in a book how you could mix something and then write with it on a hard-boiled egg and it wouldn't leave no trace on the shell. But it would leave a message on the white of the egg. He gave me the news that way until it was O.K. for me to come back."

"Well," I said. "So what?"

"So Joey had been playing with a hard-boiled egg all this week," the Canteen said, still smiling. "And I just got the idea that he gave it to you and that it's got the real cache where the four hundred grand is, safe and sound."

"My, my," I said, "a detective!"

His face snapped taut as he growled: "Cut it, Dill. You're due for a rub-out no matter what. Where's the egg?"

"I threw it away," I said.

"Did you open it?"

"Yeah."

"Then you saw the cache spot?"

"Yeah," I replied. "Let's go, Canteen. I'll die a rich man, anyway."

"No; you won't," he said and he slapped the butt of the gun across my jaw.

There was a crunch, and I saw Venus, Mars, and Jupiter all in one orbit. The force of the blow knocked me clean off my feet. I dived into a chair, knocking it in half, and I sprawled on the floor while Rose Fanta laughed hoarsely at me.

I put my hand to my cheek and it came away bloody. A drop of blood fell to the rug and made a small splash. I stared at it, my head ringing bells. I was so surprised, it didn't make me mad.

Then he kicked me in the back and I came up with both arms swinging. The Canteen stepped away and leveled the gun at my belly. The little black hole in the barrel steadied me. I lowered my arms.

"You know what I'm going to do?" he said softly. "I'm going to take off your shoes and strap you to a table. And then I'm going to get Rosie's best bread dagger and I'm going to start cutting off your toes, one by one, until you come across with the truth."

"Never mind the surgery," I replied, gasping for breath. "I'll talk."

"Then give it to me straight. Did Keel give you the egg?"

"Yeah." I felt my jaw. It hurt.

"Did you open it?"

"No."

The Canteen looked pleased. "Did you throw it away?"

"No," I said. "I locked it in my desk."

"I thought so," he sneered. "You hear that, Rosie?"

"I hear it," she said. "It sounds like Europe to me. Come on. Let's blow to his place and get it."

"Right." The Canteen nodded grimly. "And you"—to me—"are coming along, Dill. If you've lied"—he paused—"well, it won't be very nice. Not very nice—"

4

MY APARTMENT HOUSE looked like Dracula's castle when we pulled up in front of it. It was half after midnight by my wrist watch and nearly every light on the front was out, including my own. I shivered. This was Dill's last stand and no mistake. When the Canteen saw that I had opened the egg—

"Get out," he said softly. "Then stand on the sidewalk. Is there a doorman?"

"No doorman," I said.

"Good! Rosie!"

She was at the wheel with that damned wig on. "Yeah?"

"Go down the block a little ways. Keep the engine running. If you see a bull, drive off."

"O.K., Canteen." She nodded.

I got out of the car and waited on the sidewalk, facing the house. I heard the Canteen get out after me. He walked over to me and the familiar nudge of his pistol against my side stiffened me. Rose Fanta put the car in second and let it roll down the street a short way where she pulled in against the curb, the motor idling.

The Canteen looked around the street carelessly. It was so dark he couldn't have seen any one, anyway. "O.K.," he snapped under his breath. "March, Dill!"

I marched.

My jaw was hurting like the devil. There was a slight cut on the side of my face, but it wasn't bleeding any more. My cheek felt like a balloon, but so did my head.

We didn't take the elevator. The Canteen had some suspicious idea about it, so we trudged wearily up the flights of stairs to the ninth floor. When we reached the right floor, I was panting, but I could hear the Canteen puffing like an antiquated steam engine. I knew that the climb had been harder on him than me. I'd done it often before, when the elevator was out of order or being used. The Canteen was in poor condition and nothing but. And when it came to a show-down, his weariness would help all the more.

I took out my keys and opened my door.

"Step!" he said.

We went in. I snapped on the lights. The Canteen closed the door after him and snapped the bolt of the lock. He glanced around the room.

"Not bad," he said, evenly. "Not bad on forty a week, Daffy."

"Forty-five," I said. "Besides rewards."

"Rewards?"

"Yeah. For catching killers and crooks and snatchers."

The Canteen looked amused and his fishy eyes took on a beady glitter, like a snake's. "No more rewards for Daffy Dill," he said, smiling broadly. "Nothing for him but a nice white stone on his head." His voice grew sharper, colder. "Where's the desk?"

I stalled: "What desk?"

"With the egg."

I pretended to look embarrassed. "Wait a second, Canteen," I said. "Can't we talk this thing over?"

"Dill," he snapped, "stop stalling or I'll finish you here. You're through, get it? I'd be committing suicide to let you live. And all I want from you now is the egg or I'll make your dying damned unpleasant!"

The automatic was hungrily sweeping my mid-section and I remembered every story I had ever written or heard on how painful it is to get a slug in the belly. I trembled a little and said:

"O.K. Canteen. I lied."

The gun jerked a little as he tightened his hand on it.

"Don't shoot!" I said, alarmed.

His face was expressionless again. His voice sounded like a tight violin string. He asked: "Lied, Daffy?"

"I didn't put the egg in the desk," I said. "I put it in the ice box; that's all. I didn't want it to rot."

He relaxed. "Get into the kitchen, then."

We went to the kitchen and I put on the light. He stood close to me, the gun in my back.

"You get the egg," he said, "and make it snappy."

I sighed. "All right."

I went to the refrigerator and stooped down. Opening the door, I felt the cold air sweep out across my ankles. I had a box of half a dozen fresh eggs on the second tier of the refrigerator. I reached in and opened the box. I tried to make it look as though I was selecting one of them which I had especially placed in a certain spot in the box with the others. He fell for it. I could feel him leaning close to me over my shoulder, watching, and the nudge of the gun was gone from my back. He was thinking of four hundred grand at that moment and nothing else.

I selected one of the fresh eggs and stood up, closing the door. "Here it is," I said.

"Give me that," he snapped and reached for the egg, lowering his gun as he did so.

"Sure!" I said.

I rammed that fresh egg straight into his face with all the snap force I could summon.

The shell split into pieces and stuck into his flesh and the clammy yolk and albumen spattered all over him and got into his eyes.

He yelled in swift fury.

The automatic came up and blasted. But he was half blind, and I leaped away from the gun and got around behind him as his pudgy fingers clawed at his eyes, trying to push away the sticky mess which covered them.

THERE WAS A pot of water on the stove. I grabbed it and it felt heavy with the water in it. I cracked it down across his skull, and it made a resounding bong like a church bell before it was wrenched from my hand and fell to the floor, the water drenching him completely.

He fired again. The roar of the gun was deafening in the small confines of the kitchen and the bullet took my little china clock off the kitchen wall above the sink. I remember it read a quarter to one as the slug smashed it in half and dropped it into the sink.

He was half facing me, the egg still in his eyes. I crossed a jab to his jaw which knocked him across the room and he nearly fell into the sink. But the jab gave him direction. He wheeled instinctively and fired at me again.

His aim was good. The slug cut an open welt across the inside of my left leg and made me emit a groan of pain. He fired his fourth shot when he heard my voice, but this slug went over my head into the china closet where I heard glass breaking.

I dived across the room to the utensil drawer and yanked it open in one strong motion. The bread knife lay on the top of the heap, big, sharp, and comfortable. I seized it and turned.

The Canteen's eyes were opened but they were glazed. He was trying to focus, trying to find some movement on my part so that he could let go with the gun.

I picked up a glass from the cabinet shelf under the utensil drawer and tossed it across to the opposite side of the room. It smashed where it fell and the Canteen fired two quick shots in the general direction of the mess.

In doing so, he twisted around so that his back was toward me.

I ran up to him, the bread dagger in my hand. He heard my feet on the linoleum and he wheeled back in time. He could see now. He made out my body tensing. He swung the gun around for another shot and in blind desperation, I swung down the bread dagger with all my might.

It caught him across the back of the wrist and the only thing that saved him from losing his hand was the fact that the naked blade struck his coat, sliced through it, and opened a two-inch gash in his flesh which spurted blood like a geyser.

The gun dropped to the floor.

I didn't pick it up immediately. I went after him to punch him down, and I forgot that I still had the knife in my hand. He didn't, though. He saw the flashing steel under the electric light, and it took the heart right out of him. Cold steel will any time.

He screamed in terror and ran out of the kitchen. He must have thought I was going to carve him, but I didn't have any such idea. I just forgot to get rid of the blade.

I dropped it then and dived for the gun. He made the living room before I went after him with the gun in my hand.

He snapped the bolt and threw the door open. I fired at his legs, but I missed by a yard. I fired again, but this time there was only a dead click. The clip in the magazine had run out.

I swore and ran after him. He'd left a trail of blood all the way across the apartment. He lanced out through the open door, and I knew that I'd never catch up with him.

And then, from the hall outside the apartment, one single shot burst out like thunder and a man fell heavily.

I WENT TO the door. The Canteen was dead, on his back, a blue hole in the center of his forehead, and over him, service revolver in hand, stood Bill Hanley, my bosom flatfoot friend, and Inspector Halloran's best dick on the homicide squad.

"Hi-ho!" I groaned and went back into the apartment and sank into a welcome chair.

Hanley came in and put his gun away. "Daffy, you cluck," he said, "whatever made you think you could handle a bird like the Canteen?"

"I dunno," I gasped. "But, poppa, how come? How come you got here in the nick of time to save this pulsing heart? Honest, Bill, I thought he had me there."

Hanley shook his head. "I've been waiting in front of your place for the last hour," he said. "Latham told me you had been with Keel and Barber when I got to the Hideaway after some one called in to the bureau. I packed the stiff into the public-welfare wagon and came right over, but you weren't here."

Stopping a moment for breath, he went on: "I stood across the street in the shadows and waited. I saw you drive up with that doll and the Canteen. I guessed the whole lay right then."

"Did you?" I asked.

"Sure!" he said. "The Canteen bumped Barber and Keel so's there wouldn't be a split on the four hundred grand they heisted. The Canteen got you because you were the only one who knew where the cash was."

"You're to the point." I nodded. "Keel gave me a hard-boiled egg with the dope written inside of it." I got up and unlocked my desk and brought out the shelled egg. "Here's the location of the four hundred grand."

"Good!" Hanley grinned. "That washes the whole business, then. Come on down to h.q., Daffy. Halloran will want to shake your hand. Can you help me cart the corpse down or are you still weak in the knees?"

"I'll help you—" I started. Then I snapped: "Poppa! The doll! She's parked downstairs in the black sedan they used at the Hideaway. We'll have to get her first!"

"Nerts!" Bill Hanley smiled. "I handcuffed both her mitts to the steering post before I came up. Unless she's Houdini, she's still calling me a couple of so and so's. Come on, Daffy, and play undertaker with me. And for Heaven's sake, don't eat that egg. It's evidence."

He needn't have said that. Somehow, now that it was all over, I just didn't have much of an appetite.

THE MUTE ONE

The Clue of the Four Headless Snakes Lures Daffy Dill into the Room of Purple Death

1

FEBRUARY IN NEW York is like July at the South Pole. They're both frigid. From the forward deck of the dirty little tugboat we could see the S.S. *San Pedro* down the bay, disappearing now and then amidst the thick white mist that came up from the waters. The ship was at anchor, waiting to come through Quarantine.

They were all on the tug—all the laddies who cover the water front for their respective newsrags. There was Browne of the *Tribune,* MacLain of the *Sun,* and four or five others including myself, Daffy Dill, of the *Chronicle.* I was pinch-hitting for Solly Hanson, the regular water front reporter on the *Chronicle.* A bad cold had flopped him on his back in bed, and feeling one of my peculiar hunches, I volunteered to the Old Man to take the job for the day.

I was regretting it, too....

The name of the tug was the Aloha, and with a hula-hula handle like that, it was having a tough time trying to get through the cakes of ice that floated on the surface of the upper bay.

Being one of those guys who can't ski or ice-skate, but who's a whizz when it comes to riding a surf board across the briny deep, I wrapped my overcoat tightly around me, shivered at the bite of the river wind through the thin part of it at the seat, and murmured lustily:

"Hi-ho, hi-ho, it must be simply beautiful in Florida!"

Browne, of the *Tribune,* a nice enough little guy with specs, laughed and called to the others:

"Listen to Daffy Dill bemoaning Sol's sparsity! One day and he complains about the cold. Daffy, if you had to do it day out and day in for years—"

"I wouldn't last years, friend. Not with my weak heart and tender constitution," I said.

"Where's Solly Hanson?" MacLain asked.

"Sick," I said. "Listen, do you guys always take this tug out to meet incoming steamers? Why don't you wait until they land?"

"Because we wouldn't get a story then," said Browne. "Ship news is ship news, Daffy. And the home edition waits for no man's colyum. If we didn't take the tug, we'd be late for deadline."

"Yea, verily," I sighed, shivering. The S.S. *San Pedro* loomed up close to us. I pointed a shaking finger.

"Thar she blows, mates!" I nudged Browne. "Who's on board, anyway? I can't figure why we're all going down to a little tub like the *San Pedro* when the Berengaria gets in this morning. Don't tell me some one important is coming up from Panama!"

Browne ogled. "Do you mean to say you don't know who's coming in today?"

"You heard me, friend," I replied.

Browne shook his head. He said dryly, "Did you ever hear of Dr. Emerus Sheldon?"

"Why not?" I said. "Curator of mammals and reptiles at the Municipal Zoological Gardens."

"Right the first time. Two months ago, Dr. Sheldon

He grabbed the diamond from the old gent

sailed for Panama to try and bring back the first captive bushmaster to be exhibited in America. He's been trying to get one for years."

I shrugged. "So what?"

Browne sighed. "So if you read your own newspaper once in awhile, you'd know that Dr. Sheldon caught his bushmaster two weeks ago. He's bringing it in today on the *San Pedro.* And along with it, he's got a cargo of fer-de-lance snakes and a couple of vampire bats, that's all."

"What?" I exclaimed. "No movie stars? Solly is always telling about the pretty legs of the pretty movie stars who pose for his camera. I'll be mighty disappointed if I don't meet one of them during my one day on the water front. Solly was telling me he loaned two bits to Kay Francis when she came back from Europe last year. What a pleasure!"

"Listen," Browne said, "this is one of the most important

herpetological captures of our time. We are going to have a live bushmaster on exhibition in the Municipal Zoo. Dr. Sheldon captured. And you talk about movie stars! Don't you want to see the snake?"

"What for—an interview?" I grinned. "I'll bet you one fish he won't talk for publication."

Which remark brought on a despondent silence and the tug came alongside the ship. We all got up into the prow and waited for the deckhands to toss down the Jacob's ladder.

IT RATTLED OVER the side in a few minutes. We climbed it with the wind whistling through our scanties and when we reached the deck, the cruise director was standing there, a little short bird in a blue uniform and lots of brass buttons.

"Good morning, gentlemen," he said importantly. "I have a list of prominent passengers right here in my hand. If you will wait a moment, I'll read it to you and you can take your pick of whom you want to see."

"Nerts, my dear fellow, nerts," Browne said. "We know the passenger we want to see. His name is Dr. Emerus Sheldon and he bunks with a genuine bushmaster from the tropics and a bald-headed assistant with the antiquated handle of Amos Benefield. Where's his cabin?"

" 'A' deck," said the cruise director. "Cabin 4-E."

"Eureka!" Browne said, grinning. He slapped MacLain on the back and roared, "Lead on, MacDuff!" The whole mob of pencil-pushers retreated into the lounge like Napoleon's army emigrating from Moscow in the good ole days. It looked like Dr. Sheldon was holding an old home week.

I didn't go.

It was just one of those things. You know—a hunch. I looked at the cruise director's face and one hit me. He had that kind of a pan. It was lined with trenches which spelled one thing to me—worry. And worry in any man is the cause of a menace. And to a scribbler, menace is a story and just another reason why editors pay so much per week for their inane copy.

I tugged at his sleeve, trying to look sinister, and I said in my best basso profundo, "Well, friend?"

He stared at me. "Yes?"

I said softly but importantly, "My name's Holmes. Homicide bureau." I hashed a tin badge I once picked up in a pawn shop and which I carry on the back of my lapel for emergencies.

The cruise director looked stunned. "Then—but I thought you were one of those reporters!"

"Naw," I said in my best flatfoot manner. "Deteckatiff! That's me." He nodded with surprise and I knew that my hunch was right. Something had gone radically wrong on the trip up from Panama, and he was doing his best to keep it quiet and away from the news-hounds. I felt warm again, despite the trip on the ice-bound tugboat.

"Come along," he said, and I came.

He took me to his office off the main salon. He sat down behind his desk and we both lighted cigs.

He said cautiously: "I didn't expect the police until we docked at eleven. In the cable from Centre Street they said—"

I waved my hand and wondered how in hell I could break him down and find out what it was all about, without him getting wise. I said blandly:

"You know how it is! The chief thought I ought to come down on the tug and look things over before you docked. He wanted you to give me the dope first hand on this"—I took a chance and held my breath, "—this murder."

The cruise director looked horrified and leaped to his feet. I could see that my guess was wrong and that I'd put my foot in it—which same I can always be relied upon to do.

"No, no! Mr. Randall didn't die! His head was badly bruised from the blow when he was knocked out, but he recovered all right, even though the thief got away."

"Say, friend," I said, "I'm sorry. I'm sort of mixed up with another ship case coming in today. The Atlantica had some trouble. A shooting, I think. Suppose you give me the details straight."

It worked. He nodded and sat down.

"It happened two nights ago off the Carolina capes," he said. "We were all at dinner. Mr. Randall suddenly remembered that he'd forgotten his glasses. He got up and went back to his cabin, 4-E, 'A' deck."

"Which Randall is that?" I asked.

"Burton Randall," he said. "You know—the private banker. Twelfth richest man in the world."

"Oh, yeah," I said thoughtfully.

"Keep talking."

"When he got to his cabin, there was a man in it. The man was masked. He was ransacking the stateroom. He held Randall up and threatened to shoot him unless Randall told him where the Canary was."

"The—Canary?" I probed, figuring out the streamer which would blanket the *Chronicle's* page one.

"Yes," said the cruise director. "You've heard of the Canary, surely. The big yellow diamond? It's worth a small fortune. Five hundred thousand dollars, I believe."

I whistled. "Five hundred grand! Why in hell didn't he put it in the purser's safe?"

"He was afraid to," the cruise director replied. "He hid it in his own cabin. Then, of course, when this man threatened to kill him, he divulged the hide-out. The thief took it, struck him over the head and made his escape."

"Where'd he buy this Canary in the first place?"

"Private seller," said the cruise director. "Some Spanish mogul in Havana. That's where Randall and his wife joined the ship. He bought it for her." He sighed. "He didn't keep it long. You can see, of course, how this publicity would hurt us. It must not reach the newspapers."

"Of course it mustn't," I lied, conscienceless. "Lemme see a list of your passengers, friend."

2

THE SNAKE MAN

HE HANDED OVER the list and I went through it. There were about one hundred and fifty passengers. It was only a small tub. In the "H's" I nearly dropped dead. I came across the name "Jeremiah Hogan." If it was the same Jerry Hogan I knew, he'd been in the police line-up since he was a twelve-year-old. I checked the moniker mentally and went on to see what I could see. In the "L's," I solved the case as far as I had to. There was the well-known name, "Damon LaSalle."

Even a shamus could have figured the whole thing right then. Damon LaSalle was the slickest, most polite jewel thief going. He was about sixty-five. He must have been. My pappy used to tell me stories about the slick LaSalle when I wore bunting baby blue. Either Damon LaSalle had lifted the Canary, or Jeremiah Hogan, alias "Snip "Hogan, had lifted it. Or maybe both of them had.

However, that was none of my business especially. I have always looked forward to a long and healthy life, so I decided I had enough dope to write a bang-up heist yarn of the high seas. Sure I knew those two yeggs had the stone. By my job was writing, not arresting. So I ankled tactfully out of the cruise director's office and went back to the deck, just as Browne and the rest came by.

Browne grabbed me and pulled me along. "Sap, where have you been?" he hissed. "Your chief'll be sore as hell if you don't cover Dr. Sheldon. Come on! He's taking us down into the hold to show us the bushmaster and his vampire bats and stuff."

I shrugged. "What've I got to lose? I'll come."

Browne was a nice guy. He took me up to Dr. Sheldon himself. Then he introduced me. Sheldon was tall and had gray-white hair. He was smoking a pipe, a droopy bowl type like Sherlock Holmes used to sport, and he had the kindliest face I ever saw. He looked so gentle, it was hard to imagine him handling a tough viper like the bushmaster at close range.

Then I met his assistant, Amos Benefield. Like Browne had said, Benefield was as bald as a billiard ball, a squat little man with an overhanging stomach. He looked sour and he only nodded to me curtly and kept walking, cutting me nicely.

I winked at Browne and glanced at the floating icebergs in the bay. I said:

"It gets cold this time of year."

"Don't mind him," said Browne. "Nobody does." Which same seemed logical enough to me, so I didn't mind him, and finally we left the deck once again and descended stairs and stairs and stairs until we came to the hold where the wild cargo survived.

The hold was locked, of course, but we had a ship's high mucky-muck along and he saw to it that the door was instantly opened. We all trekked in, jabbering so loud, it sounded like the ladies' tea circle on Tuesday afternoons.

Dr. Sheldon was in the lead, with Amos Benefield right behind him. Dr. Sheldon led us around a lot of boxes and crates and things until we readied the spot where his snakes and bats had been stored for the voyage. We all drew around in a circle as the curator stepped forward to pull out the crate with the bushmaster and open it to give us a look.

Suddenly, Dr. Sheldon stopped. He gasped sharply, as though some one had stuck him with a knife. I got the chills a second. I thought the damn snake had gotten out and bitten him in the leg or something.

But it wasn't that.

One of the crates, with Dr. Sheldon's name on it, was pulled away from the wall. On the top slat in bold letters were the words:

Stay Away. Caution. Contents Deadly. Fer-de-lance Snakes Enclosed.

But they weren't enclosed. The whole side of the box had been ripped out with a chisel. And on the floor beside it reposed the twisted lengths of four fer-de-lances.

They were as dead as yesterday's news. Their heads were smashed to bits, apparently each by a bullet.

The queer thing, though, wasn't the smashed heads. It was the bodies of the snakes. Each one was cut in three pieces, and the belly of each one had been slit from the end of the tail to the curve of the throat, throwing organs and blood all over the floor.

Dr. Sheldon was speechless. Amos Benefield got so white with astonishment, I thought he was going to faint. Browne croaked:

"Well, what do you know about that?"

"Nothing," I said, baffled, "except that those poor little tykes did not perish from seasickness."

WHEN THE *SAN PEDRO* docked I lammed right away, going through the customs with my press card. I was going down in the elevator of the pier when I bumped into Sergeant Bill Hanley, my pal, and Inspector Halloran, my Nemesis. Halloran grunted to me and walked away. Hanley nudged me and said:

"Stick around, Daffy. There may be a yarn."

"There is a yarn. A couple of them," I said, "only I've gotten them already. I'm that way. And listen, Poppa, give me a buzz at the office when you arrest Hogan and LaSalle." Hanley stared. "What?"

"Sure," I said. "Hogan and LaSalle lifted the Canary diamond. They're on board. If Halloran arrests them, give me the tip."

"Yeah, yeah," Sergeant Hanley grunted, "but how in hell did you find out?"

"Shh," I whispered. "I read it in the stars last night through my little telescope."

"Huh?"

"Positively, I cannot tell a lie. So long, Poppa."

I left him there, all agog, and looking very much unlike an astute detective about to investigate a missing stone worth five hundred grand.

I caught a cab and rode until I came to the *Chronicle* building, an elegant edifice, built from the circulation of exclusive yarns by Daffy Dill, and a little work on the part of the rest of the staff.

When I hied buoyantly through the swinging doors into the outer corridor of the rag, I felt the sudden flash of beauty which radiated from the face that had launched a thousand tips—none other than Dinah Mason, receptionist for the newspaper, who gives me hot and cold flashes when I'm weak, and makes me propose to her every day, just to ease my blood pressure.

"Hi, sailor," she said. "And how did you like the Old World museums on Staten Island?"

"Hello, Angel-Eyes," I said, "will you marry me?"

"Did you get that seasick, landlubber?" she quipped.

"Scared-cat," I chirped. "You're evading!"

"The answer," she said, "is no—as usual. So run along and write your exclusive. I can tell by the gleam in your eyes that you've run into piracy on the high seas. Scram, lunatic."

"Them harsh words," I said, "cut me to the quick. I hereby serve notice that there'll be no more proposals."

"Until tomorrow," Dinah finished. She laughed. "Go ahead and write it, Daffy, and keep it calm and collected. Remember Solly Hanson has a staid and sober colyum. You're only pinch-hitting."

What can you do with a gal like that? I left her and breezed into the city room. The boys and girls were all working hard trying to get out the home edition, which is usually a leftover from the morning papers. But not today. I went to the Old Man's office and went in without knocking. He looked at my shining face and grabbed his telephone and called the make-up room.

"Hold the front page," he said. "Big story coming." He hung up and asked me, "What is it, Daffy?"

"How can you tell?" I marveled.

The Old Man grinned. "You would have knocked timidly before you came in." He sighed. "I suppose an enemy submarine sank the Leviathan in the lower bay?"

"Piffle," I said. "Burton Randall—*the* Burton Randall—was held up on board the *San Pedro;* knocked out, and robbed. The heisters lifted a five hundred grand stone—the Canary."

The Old Man closed his eyes. "Who else has it?"

"It's exclusive, but you'll have to cover me. I posed as a dick and got it out of the cruise director. Halloran and Hanley are covering from the police department."

The Old Man nodded. "Halloran won't say anything. Who did it?"

I shrugged. "You couldn't print it yet," I said, "but if I were editor, I'd get out all the dope I had in the morgue on Damon LaSalle and Snip Hogan. They're both on board. I told Hanley to buzz when the arrest was made."

The Old Man snorted. "Arrest?" He shook his head. "With Damon LaSalle in it? Don't be funny. There won't be any arrest. LaSalle will walk off that boat a free man."

"But the Canary—"

"Won't be on him," said the Old Man. "He's figured a way to smuggle it off. Go ahead and write the yarn. Better yet, give it to a rewrite. You're a lousy typist. How about Sheldon?"

"Doc Sheldon was in good spirits," I said, "until he took us down to the hold and we found some one had busted in and killed four of his new fer-de-lances."

"On the level?"

"You know me, boss."

The Old Man frowned. "Regular mystery ship, eh? Well, write the snake story, but don't play it up too much. Doc Sheldon's a regular guy and he doesn't want much publicity."

I lammed. I tuned in with Bradley, who's the best rewrite in the business and can turn copy out at sixty words a minute. I gave him both stories and it was about eleven-twenty when we finished. The stories went down below and I crawled back to my own desk and smoked a cigarette; waiting for some word from Bill Hanley concerning LaSalle and Hogan.

3

THE MUTE ONE

ABOUT TWELVE O'CLOCK, just when I was getting ready to partake of some java and a hot canine, my telephone rang. It was Dinah.

She said: "Call for you, maniac. Sounds like Poppa."

"I am always at home," I said, "to our sterling police force." She clicked me in.

"Listen, Daffy," Hanley said, "I've got something hot for you. In the first place—"

"Wait a minute," I said, "how about that heist?"

"No go," he said. "We searched Hogan and LaSalle and all their luggage. No sign of the Canary. And Randall couldn't identify either of them as the bird who slugged him."

"What'd you do?"

"We had to let them go. What else could we do? And boy, was that cruise director sore when he found out about your fast one?"

"Was the inspector burning?" I asked.

"Naw," Hanley laughed. "He didn't like the cruise director much anyhow. He thought it was a hot one. But listen, Daffy, this is a new yarn. Did you see Doc Sheldon this morning?"

"Yeah."

"Did you see the four dead snakes?"

"Yeah."

"Well, someone busted into Sheldon's apartment not fifteen minutes after he arrived home. He brought the bushmaster's crate with him, y'know. He wanted to make sure that snake was safe and sound before it went to the Zoo for exhibition."

"So what?" I said.

"So this bird who busted in, slugged Sheldon, and stole the bushmaster! I'm phoning from Sheldon's place. And I picked up a warm clue on the floor of the hold where the dead snakes were stretched. Come on over and I'll show you it."

"Open the door," I snapped, "I'll come through it in three minutes!"

It took me ten, really, and the poor hack-driver nearly got two tickets in the mad dash across the city. It cost me a fin to get him out of one of them, and I knew the cop for the other. At twelve-fifteen, we pulled up in front of Dr. Sheldon's hotel-apartment on East 53rd Street and I paid off.

Hanley was waiting in the upper hall outside Sheldon's door when I came up. He nodded to me and we went in. Dr. Sheldon shook hands with me. He was sitting in a chair and his head was bandaged.

"Sorry as hell, Doc," I said, "but what happened?"

The curator sighed and he must've felt pain in his head, because he winced before he spoke. "I can't explain it. I came in with the porter. Amos was with me. The porter set the crate with the bushmaster on the floor and he left after I tipped him. Amos—"

"Benefield, the assistant?"

"Yes, yes. Almost went into the bathroom to wash up and clean before we went out to the Zoo. While he was in there, a man came out of my bedroom. He had a gun. He told me to keep quiet. I started to argue with him when he struck me over the head with the gun. I couldn't have been out more than a few minutes. When I came to, Amos was holding me and saying:

"The crate is gone! The crate is gone!"

"You mean the crate with the bushmaster was gone?"

Dr. Sheldon nodded wearily. "It still is."

"And then Benefield called me," Hanley put in.

"Where's he now?" I said.

"Home," said Hanley. "At least, he said he was going home. Anything else you want to know from the Doc?"

I saw the cue. He wanted to get me alone. I shook my head and patted Dr. Sheldon on the shoulder. "No," I said. "Thanks, Doc. And don't worry. We'll get that snake back for you, dead or alive."

The curator smiled sadly. "That's what I'm afraid of," he said. "Thank you, gentlemen, and good day."

When we got out into the hall, I said to Hanley, "Can he identify the bird who hit him?"

"He said it was a short man, that's all. With big feet. He noticed the feet."

I nodded, deducing. "And what about this clue you picked up in the hold?"

Hanley passed a slip of paper me. "Take a glam at this."

I took the paper and unfolded it. It was just a thin strip,

torn out of a scratch pad. There was some scribbling on it in pencil. Just a short sentence. It read: *The Canary is in the mute one.*

I looked up and frowned.

"Whadda you make of it?" Hanley asked.

"Plentee," I said. "Yea, verily. Unless my canny mind has gone back on me, you and I are in for a bit of a reward."

"A reward? From who?"

"From whom," I corrected, wagging my finger. "From the company who insured the Canary for Randall. And at the same time, I think we can clean up the mess about the dead snakes and the missing bushmaster."

"You mean," Hanley said, "that they're both tied up?"

I crooked my fingers. "Like that," I said. "Know where Snip Hogan is parking the carcass?"

"The Grenada Hotel, at least that's the address he gave Inspector Halloran."

"Good," I said. "Let's go. We're going to bring in two snakes. One is the bushmaster of Sheldon's. And the other is Snip Hogan."

THE GRENADA HOTEL was down on West 43rd Street, just off Broadway. It started to drizzle a little when we left Sheldon's spot, so we hopped a cab. We got into a wad of traffic on Seventh Avenue, and down near the Astor Theater, another cab hooked a complacent pedestrian and the accident held us up for nearly twenty minutes. When we finally reached the Grenada, the fare looked like the war debt and my watch said one-thirty.

We went in and stopped at the desk. Hanley knew the desk clerk. He said:

"Hogan's the name I want, mister. Where's his layout?"

"Eighth floor," said the desk clerk.

"Just a second and I'll ring him."

"Never mind that," said Hanley.

"Is he in?"

The desk clerk nodded vigorously. "Oh, yes, he's in. He came in some time ago. There was another gentleman to see him."

"There was?" I chortled. "Do you remember what he looked like?"

The desk clerk grinned. "To tell the truth, I don't. He came to the desk and asked if Mr. Hogan was in. I said yes and this other fellow took the elevator right up."

"Did you see him leave?"

"No."

"And you don't remember what he looked like?"

"I see so many guys—"

"Okay. Okay," Hanley grunted. "Never mind that. Come on, Daffy. What's the room number?"

"Fifty-five," said the clerk.

We took the elevator up to the eighth and got out. We located Room 55 just like that and we knocked loudly on the door.

No one answered.

Hanley got out his service revolver. "He's in there all right," he said. "Just laying low, that's all." He tried the knob of the door. He looked a little surprised when it turned and he realized that the door wasn't locked.

We opened it and skipped over the sill.

It was a single room with a bureau, four chairs, a telephone table and a double bed.

Snip Hogan was lying on the double bed, but he wasn't going to answer any questions. He was dead.

Hanley gasped and breathed, "Murdered, by God!"

"No," I said. "I don't think so."

We went over to the bed and looked at him. He was lying in a fixed position, as though some one had picked him up from the floor and put him there. Both his arms were folded neatly on his chest.

He wasn't pretty. He was covered with an awful lot of blood. There was a film of it over his open eyes, glazed now, and there was some which had trickled down from the corner of his closed mouth, and from his ears too. His left arm was swollen twice its size, until it looked as though it would burst the arm of his coat. The left hand was discolored in the loudest deep purple I ever saw.

Hanley was ogling. "What in hell—happened—to him?"

"That," I said, and pointed to the dorsum of the left hand, where there were two flaming red dots, about three-quarters of an inch apart. "That's what happened to him. And when it happens, there isn't much you can do about it. It doesn't kill you as quickly as a slug, but it works within five minutes, injected intravenously."

"What are you talking about?" Hanley said.

"The snake bite," I said.

"Snake bite?" He gasped. "But how—you mean—"

"Dr. Sheldon's bushmaster," I said, "bit Hogan in the back of the hand and killed him."

Hanley said nothing, but he looked a bit pale. He walked away from the bed, sticking his gun in his pocket, and he stared out of the window. "Then you mean Hogan was the guy who slugged Sheldon and stole the snake?"

"Yea, verily, Pappa," I said.

Hanley asked tersely, "Why?"

I sighed and sat down in one of the chairs. "The time has come," I said, "to explain to you the whole business. The note you found explains it. That thing about: *The Canary is in the mute one.*"

"What about it?"

"In herpetology," I replied, "the mute one means the species *Lachesis muta,* which is the scientific handle of the bushmaster. Catch on? The mute one is the bushmaster, so called because it doesn't have rattles."

Hanley stared. "How'd a pencil-pusher like you know that?"

"Why," I said, "I did go to collitch once."

"Hurry up and go on."

4

DEATH'S DOUBLE-CROSS

"LASALLE AND HOGAN," I said, "pulled the job on board the *San Pedro.* Hogan did the slugging and the actual heist of the Canary diamond. Damon LaSalle engineered the thing. He's much too slick to indulge in violence himself. After they got the Canary, one of them must have fed it to the bushmaster. Get that? The bushmaster was forced to swallow the stone. That's one way of getting stolen property through the customs and police. Whoever did the feeding job wrote that note for the guy who was supposed to pick the stone up."

"Then that's why the four fer-de-lances were dead and sliced!" Hanley exclaimed. "Some one was pulling double-cross, was trying to get the Canary for himself! He went into the hold, knowing the stone was in one of the snakes, and killed them, but he missed the right snake."

"Precisely," I said. "And our friend Hogan is the culprit. No knowledge of snakedom was his, so he didn't know what 'the mute one' meant. He should have realized that the bushmaster was the only snake in the cargo large enough to swallow the stone. The fer-de-lance is too small. But Hogan, double-crossing LaSalle, didn't know that until it was too late."

"Too late?"

"Yeah," I said. "After they left you and the boat, LaSalle must have told Hogan to steal the bushmaster from Sheldon. Hogan went up to Sheldon's, grabbed the crate with the snake, and brought it back here. He was supposed to wait for LaSalle before he opened it, but he was greedy and he still had the idea of a double-x. He opened the crate. He didn't know how to handle the snake. It bit him."

"And where is the diamond now?"

"With Damon LaSalle, probably," I said. "He took it with him after he called on Hogan a few minutes ago, put Hogan in the bed there, and departed unseen with the snake and the Canary."

Hanley bit his lip and frowned. "So far so good, Daffy," he said. "But there's something doesn't fit. How would Damon LaSalle know enough about snakes to feed the stone to a bushmaster? That's out of proportion. There's another angle to this."

"Ertsnay," I said. "I've given them all."

"I think you're wrong," Hanley said. He went to the phone and called the Waldorf-Astoria. In a few seconds, I could hear the clicks of a connection. He went on: "Lemme speak with Damon LaSalle… Huh? Oh, I see. Thanks." He hung up.

"Well?"

"He's out," Hanley said. "Now what do we do?"

"We can knit," I said dryly. "Or we can figure out whether a man would walk up and down eight flights of stairs."

"Meaning?"

I chuckled and got to my feet. "Friend," I said, "follow me. When in doubt, always ask the elevator man."

We left the room, closing the door. We had a good wait before the fresh kid who ran the high-low cage came to our floor. We got in and I flashed the tin badge on my lapel.

I said, "We're deteckatiffs, kid. We want some dope."

"Yeah?" he said, wide-eyed.

"You took us up to the eighth floor a few minutes ago, right? Never mind answering. Just listen. Do you remember taking someone else to the eighth floor within the half hour before we made the trip?"

"Sure, sure," he said. "Molly Sanders and Josey Hunt came up."

"Who are they?"

"Show girls. They live on the eighth."

"How about a man?" I said. "Didn't a man come up?"

"Oh," he nodded. "You mean the little guy with the sour pan and the bald head?"

"The—bald—head!"

"Yeah. He was nervous, too. He walked down. Least, I didn't take him down again in the cage."

We hit the main floor and the doors opened. "Okay, son," I said. "Thanks." We got out of the car and walked across the lobby. Hanley nudged me into a corner and said, "Well, genius?"

"You're right, I'm wrong," I admitted. "There's another angle. But who would have thought that Amos Benefield was in on this thing?"

"I would have," Hanley said sourly. "It took a man who knew snakes to feed the bushmaster that diamond."

"You stay here," I said. "Cover Hogan's room in case LaSalle comes in. He may not know that Hogan's dead. I'll cover the Zoo and see Amos Benefield. That all right with you?" Hanley nodded and sat down. "That's all right with me," he said."

5

THE TWO-DOLLAR GUN

WHEN I LEFT the Grenada, I headed towards Eighth Avenue to catch the subway. It was the fastest way to get out to the Municipal Zoo, which is at the end of Fordham Road.

On the way over I figured that it was a pretty long trek out there and would waste a lot of time if Benefield wasn't there. I decided to telephone. It's the lazybones in me. I popped into a drug store, squeezing a thin nickel out of my jeans and dropped it in a coin box, growling the number of the Zoo's administration building.

I got the place quickly. I said, "May I speak with Amos Benefield?"

A girl answered: "Just a second." She plugged me through to Benefield's office. I heard the receiver go up and a man with the voice of an elephant said, "Yeah?"

"This is—" I paused and then continued gruffly—"this is Holmes of the homicide bureau. I want to speak to Amos Benefield."

"Yeah?" said the elephant. "Well, this is Inspector Halloran, Daffy. So you can cut out that Sherlock Holmes stuff or I'll arrest you for impersonating a newspaper reporter. What's on your mind?"

"My, my," I said. "You *do* get around, don't you? I wanted to speak to Benefield. Is he there?"

"He's here," said the inspector. "But you're too late. He ain't speaking to no one, Daffy, least of all a pencil-pusher."

"What's the matter?"

"He's dead, Daffy. Shot through the skull with a .32. And that ain't all, either. Did you see Bill?"

"He's with me," I said. "We're covering Hogan's place. So what?"

"Did he tell you about Sheldon's snake disappearing?"

"Yeah, the bushmaster. Have you got it?"

"Benefield had it," said Halloran. "It's in the office here. It's all sliced to pieces."

"Do tell," I murmured, not so chipper now. "Do you want Hanley?"

"Tell him to keep covering Hogan," Halloran replied, and hung up.

I hung up too, sort of slowly. There wasn't any sense in my going back to the Grenada and telling Poppa Hanley to do something he was already doing. My play was at the Waldorf-Astoria, and that's where I headed.

I passed a pawnshop on the way and I walked a couple of rods beyond it before the ole hunch sense got me and sent me back to the spot. I went in and up to the counter. I'd had a vision of Damon LaSalle—and of Amos Benefield shot through the head. I didn't hanker for a burial with me so young.

Only having two bucks on my person, I was cramped for style. Every gun the pawnbroker had cost from five bucks up. And he didn't know me, so he wouldn't trust me.

I finally got out of there with a nickel in my jeans and a

realistic-looking pistol in my pocket. There was only one thing about that pistol that gave me the willies. It didn't fire bullets. Get it? It had a crooked barrel and could only be used for firing blank cartridges—with which same, incidentally, it was fully loaded.

Still and all, it was better than nothing, and it gave me leeway for a sandy in case LaSalle got rough.

When I reached LaSalle's hotel, I went to the desk and said, "What floor and room does Damon LaSalle have?"

The desk clerk looked it up. "Seventh floor. Room 76. Who is calling, please?" He picked up the telephone.

"Ixnay, friend," I said. "Never mind buzzing the culprit. I was just asking, that's all. Just asking."

He looked at me as though I were Dillinger's ghost. I smiled at him and went over to the public booths. I dropped my last buffalo head in the coin slot and called the office. Dinah Mason hit the other end of the line with:

"New York *Chronicle* editorial offices!"

"This is your Nemesis," I said.

"You again!" she said. "I thought it was important. Well, what's happened to you this time? I can't always play hero when you get in a jam. Spill, friend."

"I am," I said, "about to engage Damon LaSalle in a breezy bit of repartee. Purpose to locate the missing Canary diamond and try to pin the murder of Amos Benefield on him."

"Daffy," she said—her voice trembled anxiously and warmed my aching heart—"you'll be careful? He might try to—"

"Don't I know it!" I sighed. "I just wanted you to know that I'm here and going up. In case you see my fragile body at the morgue, inform Comrade Hanley who did it and tell him to slip a couple of slugs into LaSalle just on general principles. He might get out on a trial."

"Daffy—!"

"There is also the possibility," I said, "that LaSalle will trip up. In that case, inform the Old Man that the front page will need a thorough overhauling. Keep it open. I'll be seeing you, Gilded Lily."

I hung up. I didn't feel as chipper as I sounded and I thought what a damn fool I was to risk my life for a headline. Then I stopped kidding myself. It wasn't the headline. It wasn't Benefield's murder, either. It was just that LaSalle had tried a slick crime and that I'd opened up part of it, and would be bothered for the next two weeks if I didn't open up the rest of it.

I TOOK THE elevator up to the seventh. I was the only one in the car. I got out, feeling light at the pit of my stomach and as the gates closed after me, my legs began to feel stiff. I went down the hall until I came to Room 76. I knocked.

In a few seconds, a smooth, refined voice called, "Ye-as? Who's there, please?"

"Daffy Dill," I said. "I'm a reporter. I want an interview."

The door opened. Damon LaSalle stood there, fully dressed. He glanced at me with a half-smile and fixed a monocle over his left eye. "Howja do, Mr. Dill?" he said. "I've really nothing to say, don'cha know. But if you insist—"

"Well," I said, marveling at the perfect English accent he had, "my boss sent me up to see you. That's my job."

"Of course, of course, old top," he smiled. "Do step in, then. I'll do my rugged best to help you out."

I stepped in.

Damon LaSalle was as slick a gentleman as you ever saw. He was about sixty years old and he had snow-white hair and a snow-white mustache on his upper lip. He was devilishly handsome and had a merry twinkle in his blue eyes. He was dressed in a rough tweed suit which made him look very tall.

He didn't look a thief at all. And what's more, he certainly didn't look like a killer.

He motioned me to a chair and walked to a table where there was a bottle of whisky and some seltzer. "Will you have a spot?" he asked. "Do join me!"

"No, thanks," I said. I wanted a cigarette, but I didn't light one. I kept my hands free and held my right in my coat pocket.

"I would appreciate it greatly, old fellow," LaSalle drawled in kindly tones, "if you would keep your hand away from that gun in your pocket. Guns make me nervous, don'cha know?"

I took my hand out of my pocket, flushing. "I—ah—"

"Oh, no!" he said. "Don't explain. Possibly you were frightened of my—er—shall we say—reputation? Be that as it may. I cannot help but feel the hostility of your weapon. May I ask that we conclude this interview as rapidly as possible?"

"I—ah—"

I faltered, the wind out of my sails. "I wanted to know your reaction to the theft of the Canary on board the—"

"My deah fellow," he smiled at me benignly, "last year I made public the fact that I had retired from my career of jewel collecting. The theft was quite unfortunate, and I hope the thief will be caught. As for myself—" his eyes twinkled with something grimmer than merriment—"I am still and will be permanently in retirement. And now good day."

Before I knew it, he had me up and out of the door. I stood there, feeling like a damned fool. For one of the few times in my young life, I'd been thrown off. I hadn't said what I came to say. I hadn't done what I planned to do. The way he'd treated me, I was just a little boy asking too many questions. The way he spotted my gun!

It made me mad.

I went downstairs in the elevator and loitered for a few seconds in the main lobby. I got madder and madder with myself until I felt all hopped up from my own emotion. I went back to the elevator bank and stood in a corner behind a lot of palm trees. I stood there perfectly still and just waited until I began to see red.

I'd been taken in properly—and at my age!

It must have been nearly an hour later—quarter of four as I remember—when the elevator came down to the main floor opened its doors, and emitted Damon LaSalle in all his splendor and looking every inch a duke.

I'd been watching the arrow of the elevator hitting the different floors for so long that I was groggy. But I was still mad.

He went out the Park Avenue entrance without a glance around him. He was a cool boy all right. I hiked out of the palms and tailed him.

He took a cab at the entrance and went off to the next corner of Park Avenue, where a light held him up. It gave me a chance. I grabbed the next cab, climbed in and suddenly realized I was broke.

"Where to?" asked the driver.

I screwed my mouth into a snarl, flashed my tin badge as neatly as I could, and said:

"Homicide Bureau. Follow that hack right there. The red one on the corner, and don't lose him."

"Okay," the driver said. We moved up behind the other cab. While we were waiting for the light to change, the driver said softly, "What are you after, mister?"

"Killer," I said. "Are you on?"

He grinned. "I'm on. It's been a dull day. But you ain't foolin' me none. You're no dick. You're Daffy Dill, the reporter."

"How'd you know?" I ogled.

"Hell," he said, "don't you remember me? I drove you up to the Ritz Towers the night you got Mike Cantrey for the snatch of that heiress, Clare Gordon. I read all about it in the papers next day. You shouldn't have let me in on it."

I grinned. "I just pulled the dick gag because I'm broke at the moment," I said. "But if you know me, you know I'm good for the fare so let's go—"

The light had changed. The red cab ahead of us moved off and we moved after it. My driver was hot. He knew how to keep off away from the other, so as not to be suspicious.

6

POWDER AND LEAD

LASALLE'S CAB TURNED left over to Madison Avenue, and then went uptown. At 98th Street LaSalle looked around suspiciously. I thought for a minute he was on, but my driver was up to the mark. He shot ahead of the red cab and then stayed ahead of it.

"We'll tail him from in front," he said. "You just keep an eye on him and tell me if he stops or turns off."

It worked. It was queer, following some one by being in front of them. LaSalle's hack made no turns. It kept on Madison Avenue and finally it passed us and took the lead. I kept down on the floor and made it look as though my cab was empty.

"He took a look," my driver said. "He's satisfied now, I guess. Thinks I'm empty. Oops! He's stopping. Corner of 102nd Street."

We went by and turned right. We pulled into the curb immediately, out of sight of LaSalle. I got out.

"Wait for me," I said.

"You bet," said my driver.

I ran up to the corner building and peered around it onto Madison Avenue. LaSalle was just getting his change. He tipped the driver and the hack moved away. LaSalle stood there a second without moving and looked around.

That twinkle was gone from his eyes now. And his face was harsh and tight, and not the gentle pan of a gentleman of sixty with an English accent.

He was standing in front of the inn of the three golden balls. You know—a pawnshop. And in this district, which wasn't any bed of roses, that pawnshop could only mean one thing if it were to bring a well-dressed heister like LaSalle into it.

It was his fence. The spot where he cashed in his stolen stuff.

Apparently he was satisfied. He turned quickly and went into the store. I waited about five seconds and then walked slowly down Madison Avenue to the store front. I peeked in the window. LaSalle was having a whispered conversation with the store owner, a bearded old gent with avaricious eyes. The owner listened in rapt awe and kept washing his hands as though they were wet.

Then the owner pushed aside a curtain disclosing a tiny little room with no exit. They both disappeared into it and drew the curtain, while a young punk came out behind the counter and tried to look tough.

"Hi-ho," I murmured. "Brody lived; why not me?"

I opened the door and went in, shutting it softly after me. The young punk frowned at my caution and started to bellow a summons at me, but I pulled out the blank cartridge pistol and let him look down the pretty barrel. I hissed:

"Shut up or I'll give it to you!"

He turned white and nearly fainted. He thought it was

a stickup. In the curtained room, they never heard me. I tiptoed across the store to the curtain and listened.

The bearded old gent was gasping. He said:

"Himmel! Never have I seen anything like it! But how can I—"

"You'll have to break it up," LaSalle whispered. "Cut it into smaller stones. It's worth five hundred grand, do you understand?"

"Ach," groaned the old gent. "Never could I pay you that!"

"I don't expect you to," LaSalle whispered. "You cut it up and then get rid of the smaller stones. Your take is ten per cent. We'll get the cash as we sell each stone. That'll kill chances of recognizing the—"

"The Canary," I said, yanking the curtain aside.

Damon LaSalle acted before he looked to see who I was. He grabbed the diamond from the hand of the old gent and jammed it into an inside pocket of his vest. I had a flashing glimpse of the flashing fire of the stone and my blood ran warm when I thought that I'd just seen half a million dollars at that close range.

Before LaSalle could do anything else, I snapped:

"You're covered, Damon. Both hands up high right away, or you get one in the head."

He was smart. He knew I had the drop on him at a distance of three feet, and he was sitting down. He couldn't move fast sitting down. He looked up at me and smiled.

"Oh, ye-as," he said, drawling. "It's you, old fellow, the reporter with the gun."

I said to the old gent, "Get up and get out of here and

take the punk behind the counter with you unless you like slugs."

He lammed, muttering in terror under his breath. The young punk ran after him into the back of the store. I looked right at LaSalle who had his hands up and I backed away.

"Rise and shine," I said.

He got to his feet and advanced out of the curtained room until I motioned him to stop. His eyes were glittering now, and there was no monocle to cover the left one up. He smiled coldly and said:

"Dill, old chap, you're a deuced clevah fellow. Deuced clevah! I suppose you're declaring yourself in for a cut?"

"Yeah?" I said. "No, thanks. Hogan didn't live to get his cut. Benefield didn't live to get his cut. I think I'm saving the old gent's life. He probably wouldn't live to get his cut."

LaSalle's face went taut. "Hogan was a fool. I didn't kill him. He tried to double-cross Benefield and myself. He took the snake—"

He stopped, catching himself.

"I know," I said evenly. "He took the snake to kill it and get the diamond in its belly. I know all that, Damon, old top, and it bit him because he didn't know how to handle it."

"Right," he said.

"But Benefield was bit by a bullet."

LaSalle shrugged. "The fortunes of war, poor chap." His voice went cold again. "If you don't want a cut, what do you want?"

"Just—the Canary," I said. "The whole stone, if you please."

He stared and waited a long time and his face twitched terribly as it darkened with fury. It took an effort for him to shrug. He said, "Oh, well." And he reached into his vest with his left hand.

I tightened my finger on the trigger.

"Easy does it, friend," I warned. "That hand had better come out with the stone, or—"

He brought out the stone and extended it to me with his left hand. I moved in closer to him and reached for it. It flashed so brilliantly I simply had to take my eyes off his and glance at it. I couldn't help myself.

LASALLE COUNTED ON that. He knew the stone would draw my eyes and give him a split second to work on me. His right hand was free. It flicked into his left shoulder under the coat and came out with a .32 Colt revolver so quickly I couldn't even see the action.

Before I could move, I saw the flash of flame, heard the snarling little crack of the gun and felt a red hot crowbar jammed into my left side, down low.

One thing I knew when the slug hit me. I had the Canary diamond in my left hand and my fingers were closed on it.

I held the blank cartridge pistol out at arm's length directly in his face as he fired again.

Another slug hit me, a little higher under the lung. I couldn't feel that one at all. A white cloud misted me and the only sensation I had was of my trigger finger working like hell and of the six bangs of my gun before the hammer clicked on metal. I fell to the floor on my back, dimly realizing that LaSalle had not fired again. Then a numbness gripped everything and I went out.

When I came to, I was a pretty sick laddy. I found myself in a hospital with two nurses and four doctors at my bedside. I got one faint glimpse of them, and of Dinah Mason next to them, and I went out again.

The second time I came to, I felt stronger. It was daylight and I could breathe again without any pain. I didn't feel hot, either. I talked. The nurse said I'd been seriously wounded. Two slugs in the groin. They hadn't thought I'd live. But she said it was all okey-doke now.

In the afternoon, Dinah Mason and Inspector Halloran came in. The sawbones let me talk for a little while.

"What did he do?" I asked.

"Better let me spiel," Halloran grinned. "Your cab driver heard the shots and called the ambulance. We found the stone in your hand at the hospital. We nearly had to cut your paw off to get it, you were holding it so tight."

"Did LaSalle get away?" I said.

"Get away?" Halloran said. "Hell, no! You may have had blanks in that gun, Daffy, but at half a foot, blanks are damn dangerous things. No, LaSalle didn't get away. And he'll never lift another stone, either. We got him and he talked. Here's how it happened. He and Hogan and Benefield worked together. LaSalle planned it, Hogan stole the Canary, and Benefield fed it to the snake. Hogan double-crossed and killed the fer-de-lances when Benefield gave him that note for LaSalle. Hogan didn't know what 'the mute one' meant."

"I know," I said.

"Hogan took the bushmaster from Dr. Sheldon and tried another cross, but the snake killed him. Benefield went to Hogan's and took the snake to the zoo, where it was supposed to have been brought in the first place. LaSalle was there, too. They killed the snake, got the stone, and then LaSalle shot Benefield. That's all."

"What happened to LaSalle?" I said.

"He's blind," said Halloran. "You gave him six blanks in the eyes. The grains of burning powder blinded him."

"God!" I said. I sighed. I felt tired. "How long have I been here in this corpse-crypt?"

"Two days," Dinah Mason said. She held my hand. "I missed your daily proposal, lunatic."

I grinned and asked, "Will you marry me, gal?"

She didn't say yes and she didn't say no—for a change. She leaned down and kissed me on the cheek and she said, "Well, my chickadee, you never can tell—"

And just when my chances were good, the sawbones looked at his watch and said curtly, "Time's up, please. He must rest now."

And there I was.

COCKED DICE

Daffy Dill Knew the Murderer of the Two Strangled Corpses—but He Had to Stick His Own Neck in the Strangler's Noose to Catch Him

1

WHEN THE TELEPHONE rang and knocked me out of the sweet dream I was having, which same depicted one Daffy Dill and one Dinah Mason arm and arming it before a legitimate justice of the peace, I awoke sober—for one of the few times in my life.

I groaned, stretched, and yawned, turning over to glance at the alarm-clock on my sidetable. It read nine-thirty. The horror of the whole thing began to dawn on me. It was bad enough trying to sleep above the roar of the clock's ticking which usually sounded like riveters in action.

But when some fiend in human form took it upon himself to buzz me in the wee small hours of the morning, it was too much. I picked up the handset savagely and jammed it against my ear.

I said hoarsely: "You'll live to regret this, Dracula!"

The guy at the other end snickered in such a manner that I knew it could be none other than Fusion's gift to the homicide bureau. Namely—Bill Hanley, a sergeant in Inspector Halloran's conglomeration of minions of the law.

He said: "Good morning, sweetheart. How about getting the hell outa bed and going to work?"

I sighed. "Sounds indecent, Poppa."

"What's the matter?" he said. "Aren't you pencil-pushing for the *Chronicle* any more, Daffy?"

"I am pencil-pushing," I replied, "at a raise of two bucks a week. Yea, verily, Poppa, I am now the recipient of forty-seven fish every Friday. But since I am out of the hospital a mere or bare two weeks, my fran, and while the hole which Damon LaSalle put into me with one of his favorite bullets has healed with unnatural gusto, the fact remains that the wound is still cantankerous. You catchee on?"

"I catchee on."

"The Old Man," I said, "being big-hearted and such, sternly commanded that I should get plenty of rest and that I was not to set foot in the offices of his redoubtable

The brass parrot came through the air like a bullet

newspaper until eleven o'clock each morning. And who am I to argue with the boss?"

"Who, indeed," Hanley said. I heard him clear his throat with a clucking sound and then heave a mournful sigh. "Well—too bad—"

"Hey," I chortled into the phone. "What's too bad?"

"Oh, nothing," he said. "Nothing at all. Just a little murder I thought you might want to cover for your rag."

"Murder?" I said. "What is it—a natural? Or just one of those palooka killings?"

"It's a dame," said Hanley. "And she was bumped off in her apartment down in the Village. The superintendent found her this morning when she didn't answer her bell."

"Is she good-looking?"

Hanley groaned. "What do you care? You're writing her obit—not taking her cruising."

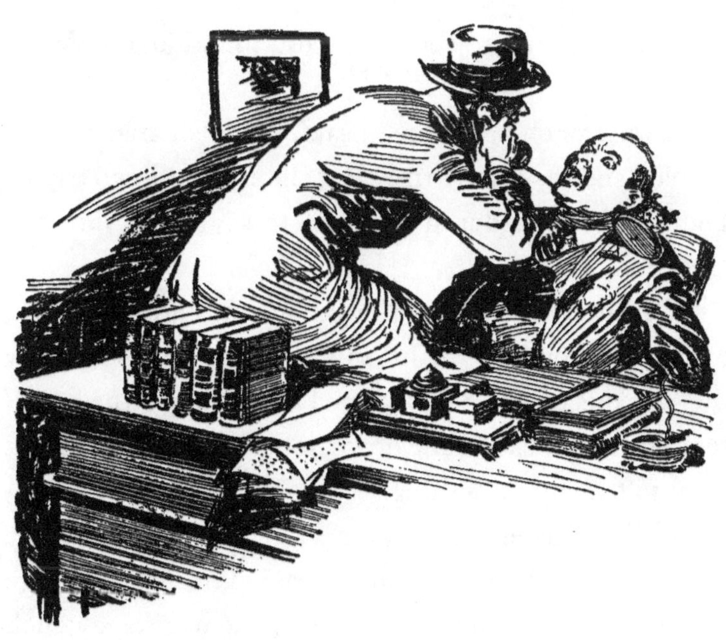

"O.K., Poppa. I'll come. Pick me up."

"Like hell," Hanley exclaimed. "Inspector Halloran nearly billed me for the gas I used picking you up on that last trip. Besides, who am I to help your swindle sheet. Pick yourself up, and then put yourself down at Number 14 Sheridan Square. You catchee?"

"I allee same catchee," I said. "I come quick, chop-chop in my ballbearing rickshaw. Keep a light in the window and don't arrest the suspicious butler—you mugg!"

I HUNG UP before he could start cussing me. I remembered that the case would probably be on the police docket and that Samson, who covers the police beat, might run down there too. There was no sense in doubling, so I called the *Chronicle.* Dinah Mason answered in the voice which is the reason why reporters marry, and which is also the reason for my bad heart and high blood pressure.

"Hello, angel-eyes," I said.

"Hello, Rasputin," she Said. "You sound joyful. Who's dead?"

"I didn't catch her name," I said. "Will you marry me?"

"No!" she answered firmly. But she added: "Keep trying, Daffy. It gets harder and harder to say 'no.' Want the Desk?"

"Why not?" I said. She plugged me through to the Old Man who growled: "Yeah?" in a voice which nearly blew the blankets off my bed. I yipped and changed the handset to my other ear. "Tone down, tone down," I said. "I just want to tell you something."

"Well, I'm listening."

"It's like this, boss. Fu Manchu was in Greenwich Village last eve, and after they cleared away the wreckage which

Daffy Dill

he left in his wake, they found a corpse in Number 14 Sheridan Square. Hanley told me it was a dame and that it might be a story. I'm covering. I thought you might tell Samson not to double up on it."

"I'll tell him," the Old Man said. "And for God's sake, Daffy, see if you can find something sensational in the bump. I'm damn sick and tired of headlining the tenseness of the European situation! Every time a king blows his nose over there, Havas sends a war dispatch. A nice juicy murder would be awful restful right now."

"I'll see what I can do," I said and hung up.

I got out of bed—painfully—and drank my breakfast. Then I dressed. In fifteen minutes, I was over at Fifth Avenue, nearly breaking both my arms trying to flag a hack driver who slept while he rode. He finally saw me and jerked over to the curb. I climbed in.

Ten minutes later I climbed out and left the cab driver to continue his nap.

Number 14 was a regular apartment house. It looked pretty respectable—so much so, in fact, that I saw sensationalism fading away. I paid off and went in. Hanley's squad car was parked in front of the building. In the vestibule, I met a gorilla in a uniform.

"Hello," I said tentatively.

"You Daffy Dill?" he growled.

"Yes, friend."

"Sergeant Hanley said for you to go right up. It's the third floor rear."

I went upstairs where I met another cop, standing outside the door to the *situs criminis* as Clarence Darrow would say. I gave him a song and dance and got inside without any trouble.

Bill Hanley saw me right away and came over. There were three other men with him, a photographer who was shooting the corpse, a finger-print man who was spreading powder all over the spot, and Doc Kerr Kyne, the chief medical examiner, who was stooping down over the body.

"How guzzit, Poppa?" I asked Hanley.

Hanley shrugged. "Damn queer thing, Daffy. Her name's Marion Mills. She's from Kansas City. We found some letters from a brother out there. We'll wire him to come on right away. The superintendent found her this morning like I told you. She'd been living here for two years, trying to paint pictures. The super said she was pretty much alone all the time. No friends, no bankroll. One of those things."

"You don't know who did it?"

"No. It was a nasty sorta job, too."

"Tell me, Poppa," I said.

"Well," he said, "she was strangled. With the belt of her own dressing gown. The bird who did it, wrapped the belt around her throat, then took one of her paint brushes and used it on the belt as a torniquet. Take a look at her."

Dinah Mason

I WENT OVER past Doc Kyne, who nodded curtly to me. He's a nice guy, but very proper, and he doesn't approve of me because I once called him a vulture. As a matter of fact, that's what he is. He's always there when somebody's dead.

The Mills girl was sitting in a low, easy chair. She wasn't bad-looking—a brunette, shingled-bob, brown-eyed, nice figure. She was in transparent silk pyjamas and she had a dressing robe thrown around her shoulders. Her white hands were fixed in a clawing position at her throat.

Her face was a mess. Strangulation does that to you. The belt, a thin blue-silk affair, was pulled deep into her flesh so that in one or two spots, the flesh overlapped the belt entirely. She didn't have a chance against a pressure like that.

Her eyes were wide open and bulging until they looked as though they'd pop into a burst any second. Her full lips were wide apart, and her tongue—all dried now—was sticking far out. Her throat was scratched, too, from her fingernails. Pretty tough way to go. I didn't like it much.

Doc Kyne said: "She's been dead eight hours, Hanley. Around midnight last night. Strangulation is all I can give you without a post-mortem. Anything else?"

"Naw," Hanley said. "Just send me the post-mortem tomorrow."

"Tomorrow," said Doc Kyne, "is Sunday."

"So it is," Hanley grunted. "Monday then. So long, doc."

When Kyne had gone and the search for fingerprints had proved pretty fruitless, Hanley turned to me and said: "What do you think, Daffy?"

I shrugged. "Look at it this way. Here you have a pair of glasses on this little table and a bottle of rock and rye. She was drinking with someone when it happened, wasn't she? There's still some whiskey in both of the glasses."

"Yeah," said Hanley. "We figured that all right. We kinda thought it might've been her lover—or something—"

"Her lover?" I said. "Why, Poppa, how naive! If she were drinking with her lover, she'd have expected him, wouldn't she? And in that case, she'd have been dressed alluringly. There's nothing seductive in that pair of pyjamas. And her hair would have been fixed. She—wait a minute." I stopped. "Where's the bedroom?"

"In there," Hanley pointed. "Why?"

"Was the bed slept in?"

"Yeah," Hanley said. "It was all mussed up and the covers were thrown back. There was an alarm clock next to it, set to ring at eight-thirty."

I said: "Did it go off? Was the alarm spring run down?"

"I don't know."

"Tsk, tsk," I said. "Let's see. We went into the bedroom and I saw what Hanley had said was true. The sheet on the bed was rumpled as though Marion Mills had lain on it. The blankets were thrown back as though she had gotten up. I picked up the alarm clock, noticing that the alarm button was pointing to ON. I tried the winder. It moved easily. The spring was entirely wound out.

"Well?" Hanley said.

"Simple, Poppa," I said, "but I'll bet you four fish you never find the bird who did it."

"Never mind that," he said. "What's your idea of it?"

"Marion Mills," I said, "went to bed last night as usual, setting this clock to wake her at eight-thirty. Sometime before midnight, some one called on her. She got out of bed and answered the call, throwing a robe over her shoulders. She let the killer in, had a drink with him, and she was bumped off before she knew what was happening. Result—the alarm went off this morning, and kept ringing because she was dead and couldn't turn it off."

"So what?"

"So this. She must have known the caller pretty well to allow him in and drink with him at that hour in her pyjamas—which as you have no doubt noticed, do not conceal much. Catchee on? In other words, if it were a gentleman friend, she would not have let him in unless she looked nice, not disarranged. And yet—it wasn't a woman."

Hanley asked: "How do you know?"

I grinned. "Don't kid me, Poppa. I know for the same reason you do."

"Oh," said Hanley. He looked inane. "You saw the cigarette then?"

"Sure," I said. "Right next to the drinks. It was a Fatima and it did not have lipstick on it, right?"

"Right," he said. "But if it wasn't a woman and it wasn't a gent friend, then who was it?"

"Her husband," I said. "Call me up when you find him.

That is—if I'm still alive. Otherwise, give the story to anyone of my four kids. So long, Poppa. Long may you rave...."

2

ON MONDAY—TWO DAYS later—promptly at eleven o'clock in the morning. I tripped merrily into the outer office of the New York *Chronicle.* I paused for a second at the door to admire the sheen of Dinah Mason's platinum hair, which rivals Harlow's any day of the week. Then I went over to her before she saw me, kissed her lustily, and then said: "Hi, toots!"

"Skip today's proposal, Adonis," she chirped, cutting me off. "There's work to be done and news to be written. In the first place, Judge Bedford has been trying to get you all morning."

"Judge Bedford?"

"In the flesh," she said. "He told me to tell you that it was urgent, and for you to get in touch with him immediately. I tried your dive but you weren't home—or else you were nearly dead from sleeping."

"Right the first time," I said. "I rose early and exercised my elbow on Bill Latham's Hideaway Club bar. There's nothing like a nice big breakfast, say I."

"Judge Bedford," Dinah said wearily, "called and asked me to tell you—"

"All right, all right," I said. "I'll get in touch with him."

I lammed into the city room and went to my desk. I didn't bother to unlock my typewriter; picking up my handset, I called Judge Bedford's law office. Bedford was a harmless old codger who had retired from the bench and who conducted a clientele of few people more for his desire to be doing something than anything else. His chief occupation was marrying eloping couples in his capacity as justice of the peace, but his rep was still good for a story with his opinion on any controversial matter, and it was during the hanging of Marie Courant, the gal who poisoned four husbands, that I first met him.

He answered in his genial bass voice: "Hello? Bedford speaking."

"Hello, Judge," I said. "This is Daffy Dill. I heard you called me. Did you get the ticket for speeding or parking? I'll fix it." I always kidded him like that because when I phoned him, it was usually for much the same thing.

"Daffy," he said seriously, "could you come over to my office this afternoon at two o'clock?"

"Sure," I said. "What's up?" He sounded worried.

"I may be all wrong," he said. "That's why I'm calling you in, instead of the police. It's just an idea I have about the Mills case."

"The Mills case?" I said. I thought for a moment. I had nearly forgotten about the gal with the robe belt for a necktie. "Oh—that," I murmured. "You mean the murder in the Village?"

"That's the one," he replied. "Marion Mills. I think I know who killed her."

"You do!" I yipped, rising from my chair. "Now take it easy, Judgie, and give me a few facts before you ring off. How come?"

"Well," he said slowly, "it's this way, Daffy. You remember I once told you that I practiced out West?"

"Yeah."

"Well, during that time, I was a justice of the peace in Kansas City. I've looked up my records, and I find that in April, 1925, I married that girl to a man named Charles Kenyon."

"You did!"

"Yes." He paused to clear his throat. "Now, Daffy, there was something very peculiar about that marriage. From what I gathered, it seemed that Marion Mills was deeply in love with Kenyon, but that her family objected strenuously to him. He had served a term in San Quentin for forgery."

"How did you know all that?" I asked.

"I knew the Mills family very well," he said. "Howard Mills, her older brother, practiced law in Kansas City. It was finally decided that Marion would go ahead and marry him. Howard Mills and his wife were the only witnesses. I performed the ceremony."

"What happened then?" I asked.

"They left immediately for the East," Judge Bedford said. "She had a sizeable little fortune of her own then—about twenty-five thousand dollars, as I recall. They wound up in Philadelphia. After Kenyon went through her money, he left her there. She wrote all this to her brother. Then she went to New York and took up her art work again—rather than return home ignominiously. She hoped to make a go of it. That was about two years ago. I correspond with Howard Mills myself occasionally. That's how I learned all this."

"But what has that to do with the girl's murder, Judge?" I said.

"Just this," he said. "Saturday afternoon around four o'clock, not much later than when the police found Marion dead, a couple came into my office and asked to be married. I agreed and married them. And it wasn't until the entire thing was over that I thought I recognized the groom as Charles Kenyon. He had grown a mustache and beard, but I am pretty certain it's one and the same man."

"Had he changed his name?"

"Of course. He'd changed his general make-up too. He calls himself Dr. Emmanuel French now. Where he stole the prefix, I don't know. And he married Mrs. Harriet de Vrie, a widow."

"De Vrie of Park Avenue?" I said.

"That's right."

"Holy, holy, holy," I said, whistling. "If you're right—then he's one cool baby. I get the lay now. He marries one gal for her rocks. When the rocks are gone, he bumps her so's he can marry another gal with rocks."

"Precisely," said Judge Bedford. "Of course, it was all very accidental, his being married by me. For all he knew, I was still in Kansas City. Just one of those coincidences, you know. I don't think he remembered me. He didn't seem to."

"Ah," I said, "I catchee on now. You've called him down to your office for two o'clock this afternoon, too."

"Yes," the Judge said. "I thought we might work on him."

"We will," I promised. "I'll be there at two, Judge. So long!"

I HUNG UP. Then I ambled into the Old Man's private office and told him what was to be told. He seemed pleased.

"Cover," he told me, "and for God's sake, don't get yourself shot up again like the last time."

"My pal!" I said, and went out to lunch.

It was about quarter after one when I tucked the last bit of my hamburger and java away. The date with Bedford was for two o'clock. I was early.

I got the jitters waiting around, and at about one-thirty, I decided to run up to Bedford's place ahead of time and talk over the situation before the bird of prey arrived. I hopped a Madison Avenue trolley and rode it up to Thirty-ninth Street, where I got off. Judge Bedford's spot was on the second floor of an old office building on the corner.

I went in and walked up the one flight to his office. There was no one around at all on the floor. I knocked on his door, but there was no answer. I knew the Judge didn't keep a secretary, and I figured that he hadn't heard the knock, so I went in without waiting.

There was a small foyer before you came to his private office. I crossed it and stepped in, throwing the door wide open.

What I saw stopped me cold.

Judge Bedford was sitting right behind his desk where I expected to see him. But he was dead as hell.

Around his throat was wrapped the whole damn telephone pedestal, handset and telephone wire. The killer had apparently grabbed that as the first thing, entwined it around Bedford's throat, and then used the handset as the stick to wield a tourniquet. It looked queer, sticking up behind his ears. His tongue was out, his eyes were open. His head was hanging back limply. He was dead all right.

For a few seconds, I couldn't breath. It hit me too hard; I hadn't expected anything like that.

Then I heard a voice. *"Number, please? Hello? Number, please?"* It scared the living daylights out of me and sent cold chills racing down the middle of my spine. It was the telephone operator's voice, coming out of the telephone behind Judge Bedford's head.

The sound brought me out of my trance—gruesome as it was. I stepped forward to the desk and circled the right side until I got behind Bedford's body. Then I grabbed the handset and yanked on it hard until I disengaged it from the wire. It took strength. That wire was wound up like a spring. After I got the handset out, I uncurled the wire. It left a raw reddish trail in the flesh, a trail that looked as though it had been burnt in there to stay like a scar. It made me shudder. Feeling goose-pimply, I put the handset to my ear.

"Sister," I said, "are you there?"

She said: "Number, please?" in the voice with a smile.

"Police headquarters!" I snapped. "Homicide bureau. And make it—"

Before I could finish, there was a soft, shuffling sound to my left, behind me, near the entrance of the office. I whirled around, sitting on top of the desk.

It happened so swiftly that I never even got a look at the guy who caused it all. The first thing I saw was a brass parrot, a screwy sort of bookend which Judge Bedford had used on the top of his bookcase over against the wall.

That brass fowl came at me like a bullet and it looked almost as if it were really dying!

It hit me squarely on top of the head over my eyes with

a crash that reverberated in my ears for weeks. I went over backwards, dropping the telephone. I hit the floor without feeling. Dimly, I heard the door slam, and only then did I realize that Bedford's killer had been in the office all the time and that he had been hiding behind the door which I had flung wide open so blithely when I first came in!

After that it was bye-bye and pleasant dreams for me.

3

I BEGAN TO realize that I was back in this cold world once more when I felt someone having the time of his life slapping away the side of my face. I struggled within myself to speak and when I did, it came out in a hoarse croak: "F'God's sake—lay off!"

I opened my eyes and things began to clear. The first thing I saw was the homely but honest pan of Bill Hanley. He kept saying: "Come on, Daffy, you're all right now. Come on, Daffy—"

"Cut it out," I said. "You'll have me hypnotized." I rubbed my head and groaned. Then I stared at Hanley.

"Gee, Daffy," he said, "I'm sorry, but I had to bring you outa it. You was dead to the world. How do you feel now?"

"Lousy," I said, "but I'll live. Did you see Bedford?"

"Yeah," said Hanley. "I wanted to talk to you about that."

"O.K.," I said. "But let's talk in a squad car. We're going down to headquarters. I can tell you this much right now. The guy who killed Bedford is the same mugg who strangled Marion Mills on Friday night. You savvy?"

"I savvy," he said. "Let's go."

We went downstairs into Madison Avenue, Hanley holding me by the arm. It's surprising how you get a jag after a bump on the skull. You feel tighter than a kite.

We crossed the sidewalk to a squad car and got in. "Far

be it from me, Poppa," I said, "to inquire into the business of the police—but how in hell did you happen to come there?"

Hanley said: "You telephoned."

"Sure, but I was konked before I got you!"

"I know," he said, "but the operator put the call through anyhow. She said she heard groans. We traced the number and location and I came right out."

"Well done, my lad," I said, as he started the car, put us in gear, and made a full turn at the corner to head downtown again, on Madison Avenue, the siren going full blast. Right then, I got an idea. "Wait a second," I said. "Take me to Park Avenue and Forty-fourth."

"O.K.," he said. And after he had turned: "What's the idea?"

"The guy who bumped Bedford was Charles Kenyon, formerly Marion Mills' husband, who also bumped *her*," I said. "His motive in killing the girl is vague. It boils down simply to the fact that he wanted to marry someone else and a divorce mess would have killed the chances, get it?"

"Keep talking," Hanley said.

"He killed Bedford," I explained, "because of one of those damn coincidences that are always happening to nice people. Bedford was the judge who married Kenyon to Marion Mills out West in 1925. Kenyon must have realized that Bedford recognized him as the same man; he also must have realized the Judge had an inkling as to Marion Mills' murder. Bedford, apparently, was the only man in New York who knew him as Kenyon—a forger who had served a term in San Quentin. He knew Bedford could lead the police to him. Presto, throw another corpse on the fire!"

"I see," said Hanley. "How'd you get knocked?"

"I surprised Kenyon in the office but I didn't see him. He hid behind the door until I called you. Then he hit me."

"Well," said Hanley, "what now?"

"Now," I said, "Daffy is going to repair to the haunt of the forger. Under the guise of Dr. Trench, he is lolling in the sumptuous abode of Harriet de Vrie, all young and handsome as a bridegroom. I get out at Forty-fourth. You go to h.q., you look up your records, you get all the dope on Charles Kenyon that you can. I'll see you later."

HE STOPPED THE big squad car at the curbing and I got out, "And don't forget to let me know," he said. "This is my arrest, damn it, not yours. You can write the yarn just as well if I make the killing. Remember you're no Hercules after LaSalle's bullet hole."

"Sad but true," I said. "Sit tight." I watched him turn and head towards Centre Street. I stood there serenely for a few seconds. Then I went into a drug store and called the *Chronicle.* I gave them the entire yarn of Judge Bedford's murder.

When I finished that, I looked up Harriet de Vrie's telephone number in the directory and gave the spot a buzz. A maid answered with: "Who iz thees?"

"Fifi," I said, "this is that redoubtable member of the Fourth Estate, the New York *Chronicle,* calling you through the medium of myself, one John Doe, to ask to speak with Mrs. French, *nee* Harriet de Vrie."

"You weesh to spik with the *Madame?*" the maid asked.

"If you'll be so kindly," I said.

There was a click and a wait of a few moments. Pretty soon, the de Vrie dame was on the line.

"This is the *Chronicle,* madam," I said, business-like. "I have learned of your marriage to Dr. Emmanuel French and I called to learn what your future plans are."

"You newspaper reporters!" she said in a soprano screech of hilarity. "You *do* find out everything. You *simply* do!"

"Yes, madam," I said. "We simply do. But your plans? You see—our society editor is *simply* crying her eyes out waiting for this story about Harriet de Vrie!"

"How *sweet* of you!" she chortled. "You may say that I am *thrilled* over my secret marriage with Dr. French and that we are leaving tomorrow on the Caledonia for an extended cruise around the world."

"Isn't that ducky?" I said. "And Dr. French—I suppose he is a scion of the Punxatawney Frenches?"

"Oh, no," she said. "He is of the Philadelphia Frenches."

"Thank you so much," I said, and hung up. I stood in the telephone booth for a few seconds and did a lot of heavy thinking. In the first place, it wasn't reasonable that a guy would murder two people simply to marry another woman. It wasn't reasonable—even if the other woman had more money than the government deficit. Somehow, he could have worked his points and married the old ostrich without killing.

There, he must have *had* to marry her in a hurry; and the only way he could have married her in a hurry was to kill his first wife, in order to avoid bigamy and exposure. Bedford, of course, had only been killed as a follow-up, to cover the first crime. That was plain.

So it all came back to this. Kenyon, alias French, had married Harriet de Vrie because he needed money fast. I was pretty satisfied I had the motive. But that was all

I had. There was no evidence—not even a bit of worthwhile circumstantial evidence. What if Hanley did find the dope to prove that French was Kenyon and was married to Marion Mills? I was betting that Kenyon had a pretty good alibi for that night. There was only one wedge.

If I were able to identify him as being in Judge Bedford's office after Bedford was found dead, it was a pretty sure thing that the D.A. could wrap him up for Death House delivery, providing they could prove his past criminal record.

I left the drug store and went out onto Park Avenue. Harriet de Vrie lived at 1109, a spacious dive with two doormen, a couple of busboys, and a canopy to the curb that would have knocked your eyes out.

One of the doormen, a big bird with the build of a longshoreman, was standing out under the canopy, all dressed up in a regalia that made him look like the commander-in-chief of the Imperial Chinese chop-chops. I sauntered up and gave him a grin.

"Hello, my fran," I said.

"Scram," he said coldly.

"Listen," I said, ignoring the invitation, "does Dr. French live here with Mrs. de Vrie?"

The doorman gave me an Antarctic stare. "What's it to you?"

I flashed my lapel back at him. He got a swift look at the silver badge I had there—which same I once procured from Benny's pawnshop on East Fourteenth Street—and he paled a trifle. "Oh," he said in a small voice.

"The handle," I said, "is Holmes, Homicide Bureau. I'm going to stand right over here by this drug store. I'll be looking in the window. When Dr. French comes out—say, by the way—is he here?"

"Yeah, upstairs," said the doorman. "He came in a little while ago."

"Good," I said. "When he comes out, you give me the high sign. And, brother—if you steer me on the wrong guy, I'll turn you in for aiding and abetting a fugitive from justice."

"Don't—worry," he gulped.

4

IT WAS ABOUT a quarter of four when I saw the doorman give the sign. I faked a stare into the drug store window, and watched the entrance of the apartment out of the corner of my left eye.

Almost simultaneously, Dr. Emmanuel French stepped out from the doorway, nodded to the doormen, and climbed into a red taxi which was parked by the curb.

He was dressed to kill. He had on black trousers with a fine white stripe in them, a black suit coat, a black derby with a silk ribbon, and the other stuff went on: wing collar with a tie like the midnight sun; a pair of white gloves; a cane; and spats.

He was a handsome cuss too, with a thin sort of face, nice eyes, and a black mustache on his upper lip, skirted by a neatly cut black beard on his chin.

I skipped across the curb to a yellow cab which was parked right behind French's. I climbed in and said: "Follow the boy in front of you, buddy, but be discreet."

The chase led across Forty-second Street to Sixth Avenue where the red hack turned right under the elevated structure and then proceeded uptown. These were more familiar haunts to me. We passed the World's Fair Museum near Forty-fifth and then the red hack made a left turn and pulled up to the curb. I stopped mine, got out, and paid off.

Dr. French—after he left his hack—hiked jauntily down the street towards Broadway. I followed him, making tracks with care but he never even looked around. When he reached the gaudy canopy of the Town Club, right near Broadway, he stopped briefly, and glanced up at the name.

Only then did he glance around—swiftly at that—before he went in.

The Town Club—lest you forget—is the hot spot which is run by Jimmy LaVerne, the squarest white man in the rackets I ever wrote a squib about. It was a swanky dive with a front of dancing and liquor. But if you knew the secret password and the ropes, you could go back of the main room and come into the nearest thing to Monte Carlo we have in the metropolis.

LaVerne made his real cash from the gambling machines in the rear. The liquor concession and dancing made their way, but gambling was always the main event at the Town Club. A house is bound to win in the end no matter how you look at it. And Jimmy LaVerne played his wheels and his dice on the square, taking his losses when he got them, making his wins honestly. I'd never cracked down on him in the paper because of that. I liked him. He stood me.

I WENT INTO the club after Dr. French and climbed the stairs to the second floor where there were a couple of dancers making a feeble stab at the carioca, Broadway style. When I got there, French had disappeared. I tossed my chapeau to Lucille, a cute doll who runs the hat-check counter. I said: "Hello, Garbo."

"I ain't seen you in days and weeks, Daffy," she said. "You don't come around like you usta."

"Didn't you read about it?" I said. "I was shot up—in

the hospital for a month." I forked a one-spot out of my jeans while she looked sad, and I waved it in front of her nose. "It isn't a fortune," I told her, "but all you have to do is answer one question."

"Shoot," she said. She grabbed the bill.

"Where did Dr. Emmanuel French go?"

"Ah," she said. "On the prowl, eh? He went into Jimmy's office. I think it's a payoff. He's been hitting the Town Club nearly every night and from the tips he gave me when he left, he's been losing."

"Thanks," I said. "Forget I asked you."

"You know me, pal," she said. "I've kept my job for years."

I smiled and went over to the bar, where I could watch LaVerne's office door while I crooked the right arm. I ordered an Old-Fashioned and I had half guzzled it when suddenly the door opened. I threw off the rest of the shot in a leisurely way and watched. Sure enough, Dr. French ambled out all smiles and happiness.

I thought for a second that he was going to leave without giving me a chance to check on him. I'd have had to follow him right off, you see, and I wanted to find out why he was there. But he didn't get his hat. Instead, he turned and headed for the back room where the wheels and dice were. When he had gone in and the door closed, I left the bar and went back to Lucille.

"Gal," I said, fishing out another buck, "you're going through my roll like a goldie, but I want another favor."

"Sure," she grinned, pushing the dollar back. "But never mind the grease, Daffy. Once is enough, even for a friend."

"Thanks," I said. "Get this. I'm going in to see Jimmy. You just saw French go into the gambling rooms. If he should come out and leave while I'm still inside, let me know right away, savvy? I'm tailing him and I don't want to lose him."

"Consider it done," she said.

Then I crossed the dance floor and knocked on LaVerne's door. There was a short wait. Finally he called: "Come in!"

I opened the door and went in. "Hello, Jimmy," I said. He looked just the same as ever. What hair he had was white, his face was genially ruddy, and he had the usual Corona between his lips, half-chewed to bits. He stuck out his hand.

"Glad to see you, Daffy," he said. "Sit down."

I hit the chair in front of his desk and stretched out my legs. He went on: "How are you feelin', kid? Read about your stopping that slug. You did a neat job on LaSalle for an amateur."

"Coming from you," I said, "that's a compliment. Thanks."

He nodded absently and then scowled at me. "Well—what're you puttin' the bite on me for this time."

I took a deep breath. I said: "Jimmy—I want to know what Dr. French just saw you about."

HE STIFFENED A little. "That don't sound like you, Daffy. In the first place, that's his business and mine. In the second place, I'm no welcher with guys who square off their debts. You know that." He sounded grieved with me.

"Jimmy," I said, getting to my feet, "here's my hand." I took off my hat. "See that bump on my skull?"

"Yeah."

"This afternoon," I explained, "some rat bumped old

Judge Bedford. You'll read about it tonight. When I found Bedford dead, the rat got me with a bookend and lammed."

"Yeah?" He sounded more interested and his eyes glistened.

"Now," I said, "remember that Mills murder in the Village? You read about it Saturday in the *Chronicle.*"

"The strangled doll?"

"That's the one. The same guy who konked me, and bumped Bedford, tied the tie around the girl's throat."

LaVerne chewed his cigar. He asked in a strained voice: "But what has French got to do with it all?"

"Everything," I said. "That's on the level, Jimmy. I know."

LaVerne got to his feet and stared out of the window for a second. I heard him mutter: "So that's how he got it." Presently, he turned to me, his face looking grim. "Daffy," he said, "French has been playing the Town Club for the last month steadily. And for the last month, he's lost his shirt. When he went through his money, he asked if I'd take his I.O.U." He paused. "You know my rule on that point. I hate a welcher. I told him. I'd take his I.O.U., but also told him that if the markers weren't taken up by a certain date, it meant one thing."

"Cocked dice," I said.

"Call it that if you want," he said. "If welchers don't pay an I.O.U. with the Town Club, they ride out into Westchester—and they don't come back. It's cocked dice all right. And any boy who hands me an I.O.U. knows all about what happens if he doesn't pay."

"How much was French in for?" I asked.

"Twenty-four grand."

I whistled. "I.O.U., eh? And when was the deadline for the payoff?"

"Day after tomorrow. I was talking to my boys about him today before he walked in. He gave me a check for twenty-five grand. It was good, too, signed by that Park Avenue dame, de Vrie, who's been in once or twice. It cleared the debt. I gave him the extra grand in cash."

"He's spending it in the back room now," I said. "Well, Jimmy, that finishes the whole thing up. I've got his motive plain as day now. Can I use your phone?"

"Sure. Grab it."

I picked it up and called Centre Street. When I got the homicide bureau, I asked for Hanley. I had a wait of a few seconds. Just before I got him, the door burst open and Lucille looked in.

She said: "He's leaving now, Daffy. I'm stalling him. You'd better make it fast. He feels pretty good. He just won a grand." Then she bobbed out of the door and was gone.

Simultaneously, Bill Hanley said: "Hello?" over the wire.

It was a spot. For a second, I didn't know what in hell to say. Grimacing at LaVerne, I snapped: "Poppa! This is Daffy! Ride like hell to the Hideaway Club and get further instructions from Bill Latham in his office. Check?"

"Check," said Hanley serenely, and hung up.

5

WHEN I HIT the sidewalk under the Town Club canopy, I saw Dr. French just climbing into a cab which was standing in the front line next to the curb. He said: "1109 Park Avenue," to the driver, and sat on the cushions. He leaned forward to close the door.

I stepped right across to the curb and jumped into the cab beside him. My right hand went down around the pipe in my left pocket and I jammed it hard against his side. "Hello, doc!" I said cheerfully, and under my breath: "The Hideaway Club, you rat, and act as though you like it."

He went white and licked his lips. His eyes stole down to my left pocket. I gave him a jab for good measure. "It's a rod," I said.

He tapped the glass window with his cane nervously. The driver turned around. French said: "I've changed my mind, driver, take us to the Hideaway Club instead."

"O.K.," the driver nodded.

I reached forward and closed the glass partition. Then I eased up on the pipe and sat back on the cushions, watching French like a hawk. He asked, gulping; "What is this—a heist?"

"You mean a holdup, doc. Remember, Park Avenue doesn't say heist for holdup like the boys at San Quentin do."

That hurt him. He stiffened like an icicle and tried to move away from me, but I went after him with the pipe. "Cut out the scare," I growled in my best Capone manner, "and let's get to business. Recognize me, doc?"

"I—never saw you—before in my life!"

"Don't give me that," I snapped. "You know me all right. And I know you. You're the guy who hit me with the bookend right after you killed Bedford this afternoon."

"You're—crazy—"

"Yeah?" I said. "You don't think so. Me—I'm no squealer—*if*—there's something in it for me. Catch on?"

French bit his lips, and his little mustache twitched. "You're trying to blackmail me!"

"Trying to! That's a laugh. I *am* blackmailing you, rat. You bumped Bedford and I'm the guy who can prove it."

"Yeah?" He eyed me speculatively. "How good is your word against mine?"

"Fair," I said. "It wouldn't hurt to find out. Want me to head for Centre Street—or do we play ball?"

"How much do you want?"

"Ah, no, doc. Not in public. We'll have a nice private room at the Hideaway to discuss our—business. You're a smart boy."

A few minutes later, the hack slid over to the curb and the driver said: "Four bits. Here's the club."

Dr. French paid off. His hands were shaking too. I gave him a feel of the pipe again and we moved into the club. I felt nervous myself. Hanley's squad car was nowhere in sight.

When we got inside, I relaxed on the pipe and nudged him. "Listen," I said, "I've got to see a guy. You wait right here, see? I know your handle is French, and I know you're married to the de Vrie dame. So don't try to skip or I'll have your name on the teletype all over the country."

"Don't worry," he said. "I'll stick."

"Smart." I nodded to a waiter. "Get a private room for us. You can pay off upstairs, just the two of us alone."

"O.K.," he said. A funny kind of a gleam came into his eyes and I sighed thankfully, cause he had caught onto the idea at last. I left him and went into Latham's office. You remember Bill Latham. He's the prop of the Hideaway—and a giver of free drinks when business is hot. "Hello, Daffy," he clipped. "What's the bad news?"

"I'm playing with a killer," I said. "I'm taking him up to a private room. Hanley'll be along any minute. When he arrives, send him up to the one your waiter gives us. Tell him to listen at the keyhole. When he hears what he wants, tell him to bust in. Got it?"

"Got it," Latham said soberly. "Watch yourself."

Outside again, I collared the waiter. "Your friend is upstairs, sir," he told me. "Room 4. He's waiting for you."

"Right," I said. "Now you tell Latham that room number and then you bust it upstairs and keep your ear to the door. You're being a witness and I want you to hear everything. Get it?"

"I'll be right along."

I climbed the stairs to the second floor balcony and went along the aisle until I came to the closed door with the Number 4 on it. I grabbed the pipe in my pocket again and went in, shutting it firmly behind me.

DR. FRENCH WAS seated at the table, looking very glum. He had his head in his hands and I saw that his cane—

which same had worried me—was safe in a far corner of the room. At the sound of the closing door, he jerked, and looked up sharply.

"It's only me," I said.

He nodded and sat back in the chair. I took the one opposite him and sat down. He said: "Can't we talk this over peacably? Must you hang onto that gun?"

"Sure," I said. I put both of my hands on the table, knowing that he wasn't heeled. He wasn't fool enough to carry a rod and be nicked by the Sullivan law when he was in the clear. "That better?"

"Much," he said coldly. "Now what do you want?"

"Brother," I replied, grinning, "I've got you in the palm of my hand. You killed Judge Bedford. The cops'd give a lot to know that. You're going to give me a lot to shut me up."

"Suppose I deny it?"

"Cocked dice, my friend. You sure killed him all right." I shook my head. "Boy, you nearly killed me too, with that bookend. You're a killing fool! I wouldn't be surprised if you didn't bump that gal in the Village last weekend."

That shot him straight up in the chair like a bolt. He eyed me sharply, and I made out that I was only kidding. "Well," he said crisply, "let's have it then. How much do you want?"

"Ten grand," I said easily.

"Good God!" he exclaimed. He got to his feet and appeared to think, striding back and forth and holding his chin in his hand. "That's a lot of money."

"Sure," I said, "but your wife is rich. After all, it's cheap for covering murder. I'm an accessory after the fact once you pay it."

"I suppose it is cheap for covering murder," he said slowly. "Well—I don't know—" He tried to act it through. All the time, he was edging around the table with his strides. "I don't know," he kept murmuring. I just sat there and let him rove. I was waiting for him to get it over with. I knew he'd put his foot in it sooner or later.

Finally, in his pacing, he got behind my chair. I heard a swish and I knew it was coming. In a flash, his black belt from his trousers flung around my throat. If I hadn't expected it, he'd have had me sure. As it was, I just got my left hand up to my neck in time.

The belt tightened like a vise. The only thing that kept me from choking to death was the fact that I had my left hand *inside* the belt and the leather would have to cut through my wrist before it could reach the old Adam's apple.

He grunted and struggled to tighten that damn thing and I let him go on for a bit. Suddenly it got serious. He had the belt so tight, my own fist began to slowly strangle me.

I leaped to my feet. The party was over, Hanley should have been there but wasn't, and I had a killing maniac on my hands. With my left fist wrapped up in the belt, I was on the short end. I tried to turn but he dug the belt deeper.

I couldn't yell or anything. My left hand was too tight against my voicebox. For a moment, I thought I'd overplayed my hand and that he had me. With my right foot, I kicked at my chair.

My heel caught it and sent it spinning away from between us. He strained and put his whole weight on the belt. At the same time, I jabbed backwards with all my strength and caught him square in the belly with my right fist.

He hadn't expected it and it drained all the fight out of him like tickling will do. Just a brief second, you know. He reached for his bread basket, bending down a little and screwing his face up at the shock. I spun around on my heels. My left fist was still caught in the black belt noose, but my right one was swinging like the rotor of an autogyro. The point of his chin looked like a gigantic bull's-eye to me. I hit it and made the snappiest-sounding crack a knockout ever recorded.

It looked as though his skull whizzed around on his shoulders and after the second bounce, he laid still on the floor.

I WAS AS weak as ginger ale. I plumped into a chair, breathing hard and holding my side where my old bullet hole was. It throbbed and hurt me. The door burst open and the waiter looked in. "I heard everything!" he cried. "Are you all right?"

"Just—ducky—" I croaked, catching my breath.

Right after the waiter, Bill Hanley breezed in like a cyclone out of Kansas. He was red as a boiled lobster and breathing hard. "O.K., Daffy?" he yelled. "Here I am!"

"Think of that," I said. "Here you are and there he is and here am I—with a sore throat. He nearly killed me."

"It was a traffic jam," Hanley said apologetically.

"I heard everything," the waiter said. "I'm a witness."

So that's the way it had to be when they made up the indictment. Funny thing about French's trial though. Despite direct evidence on my part, on Hanley's part, and on the waiter's part—the son-of-a-gun actually beat the charge of murdering Judge Bedford!

And when they tried him for the Mills girl's murder, and the D A. dragged out a lot of moth-eaten circumstantial evidence that wouldn't have convicted Dillinger—that jury of farmers actually brought in a "guilty of second degree murder," and gave French, alias Kenyon, a nice scenic ride up the Hudson to Warden Lawes' sanitarium instead of the chair!

What a life!

A SLUG FOR CLEOPATRA

Daffy Dill Proves That a Man Can Be in Two Places at Once When He Follows Double Murder Along a Fantastic Trail

1

DINAH MASON, WHO is why I pay my doctor for high-blood pressure, glanced at me from her reception desk in the outer office of the New York *Chronicle,* as I dragged my young frame through the swinging doors, trying to figure out some way to live without the exertion of breathing.

"God's gift to the Fourth Estate," she said buoyantly, "is exactly an hour and thirteen minutes late. And how have you been, Mr. Dill?"

"Fair," I croaked, "except that my leprosy is bothering me." I stared at her, nonplussed. "How do you do it?"

"Do what?" she asked.

"Get here all nice and energetic," I said. "I wined, dined, and danced with you until three-thirty this A.M. Yea, verily, I might even say that you debauched with more vigor than I. Yet here you sit—with the rising sun—to gloat over me as I trudge in emaciated and undone. How do you do it?"

"Undone!" she jeered. "I like that! Listen, toots, I just get up when my alarm clock goes off instead of turning over and tossing it out of the window. You ought to try it sometime."

"Viper," I said sourly, and started for the city room. I paused at the door and flung back: "Will you marry me today?"

"Do elephants lay eggs?" she asked sweetly.

"Ah, well," I sighed, "that's that." And I massaged the end of my nose with my right thumb and went into the city room. It was all bustle and activity there, as befits a newspaper in the throes of a home edition. Disregarding the dirty cracks which several pencil-pushers made about my promptness, I trekked wearily to my desk and found a slice of paper jammed savagely in the carriage of my typewriter. "Hi-hi," I said. "An epistle...."

I picked it up and read it. It said: "See me."

Which—terse as it may seem—painted a picture of the Old Man, squatting anxiously behind his desk like a bald little goblin, and waiting to hand me merrie, merrie hell for being late.

Dispassionately, I hied myself to his private office and knocked hollowly on his door so that I could soften the shock of my actual arrival. The Old Man called, "Come in," so I went in, trying to look pale and wan, and generally about to pass away.

I said hoarsely: "Hello, boss."

"Why, Daffy Dill," the Old Man leered, "imagine seeing you here so early!"

I said: "It's this way, boss. Last night—"

"It's bad enough," he cut in, "when you try to act like a reporter. But when you try to act like an actor—" He raised his brows and indicated that there was a bad odor in the room.

"O.K.," I growled, huffed. "Give me the worst."

"I am merely giving you," he said, "an assignment. I must remind you that you are working on a newspaper and that each morning reporters are handed assignments. Do you understand?"

"When you speak English, I do."

"At eleven o'clock this morning," he continued, unscathed, "an individual by the name of Mordini—by the way, have you ever heard of him?"

"You're killing me," I said. "Who hasn't? Mordini is an escape artist like Houdini was. I guess he's the number one escape artist of the country nowadays."

The Old Man looked surprised. "My, but you're up on current events. That's right, Mordini is a famous escape artist. As I was saying, this morning at eleven he will attempt one of the most daring tricks ever tried. He is going to be sealed in an aluminum coffin and allow himself

Bill Hanley leaned down over me

to be lowered into the Harlem River off a pier around 149th Street. He will stay under water for three hours and return to this life at two o'clock this afternoon, well and unharmed."

"He's screwy," I said.

"Mayhap, mayhap," said the Old Man, "but he is going to do it and that is one stunt you can't fake, because there'll be plenty of witnesses to watch. I want you to cover it. And if he does it without killing himself, if he really stays under water in a coffin for three hours, give me a hot feature on it."

"Yea verily," I yawned. "Is that my day?"

"No," he said dulcetly. "If you don't mind, I have a little something else. Did you ever hear of Sylvia Calmette?"

*"Pul*eeze," I grinned. "The gal with the legs that fifty million Americans cry for? The star of *Burning Sands?* Superlative Pictures owns her."

"Right again!" The Old Man gaped at me. "My goodness, Daffy, but you're getting smarter. Superlative Pictures owns her. Not only that, they have her in their New York studios up at 150th Street near the spot where Mordini is going to be lowered into a watery grave for a couple of hours.

"Go over to the Superlative studios and get an interview with Sylvia Calmette. How she likes New York and the rest of the hokum. Get her reaction on Mordini's descent into *aqua pura* if you can. She's his—er—paramour, you know."

"Tough," I sighed. "O.K., boss. Is she making a picture?"

"Yeah *Loves of Cleopatra* is the opus. If they get hard, promise them some free publicity. But get a story from her. The two features will look sort of nice together."

"I get it."

"Then," he finished, "you dash back to Pier 64 and be there when they bring up Mordini's coffin. If he's dead, telephone. If not, come in and write it yourself. Now beat it."

"How about a raise?" I asked.

The Old Man stared at me for a minute, then sadly shook his head.

"And they hang pictures," he said.

2

I DIDN'T HAVE a bit of trouble getting onto Pier 64 when I finally climbed out of my hack, paid off the driver and made a mental note of the robbery for the swindle sheet which the Old Man would probably disallow anyway. Apparently it was a free show for all because the cops weren't holding anyone back.

Then, out of the curious faces, an honest beefy pan emerged and I ran over to shake hands with Detective Sergeant Bill Hanley of Inspector Halloran's homicide squad who was just as surprised to see me as I was to see him.

"What are you doing here?" I asked.

"Oh," he said carelessly, "just watching."

"Like a fox," I replied. "Don't tell me Halloran has made you come up to stop the show! I want to see this thing. I don't believe it can be done. It isn't every day you see a guy commit unintentional suicide."

Hanley sighed. "Listen, scribe, I'm not gonna stop anything. Mordini got his exhibition license and it's all legal. I'm just sticking around to call the wagon—in case."

"And you'll call it too," I said. "Tell you what, I'll bet you five fish that he doesn't stay under water three hours."

"I'll take you," he said.

Not finding anyone we could trust with the stakes, we

both clung to our own money. There was a rising shout from the crowd as two guys pushed their way towards the end of the pier, followed by another bird with a blowtorch in his hand and a can of something under his arm. The first palooka was the barker, in a brown derby and with a stogie a mile long jutting out from between his teeth. The second man was the Great Mordini.

I was taken when I saw him. I don't know what I expected, but he wasn't it. He was a runt. Not more than five feet five inches, he was thin as a minute and wiry too. He didn't have a hat on, and his coal-black hair had a sheen that hurt my eyes. He was handsome, too, in a gaunt sort of way, but, on the level, I didn't see why Sylvia Calmette should keep the home fires burning for him. He wasn't a stunner like she was, and he didn't have half the personality. He looked scared.

He went right by us, pale and uneasy, and Hanley followed so I fell into line. We all reached the end of the pier, where a huge chunk of canvas was covering something on the end. For the first time, I saw the bent arm swung out from the pier with block and tackle and I realized that this was the thing to lower the coffin into the drink.

THE CROWD CAME in closer and a couple of flatfeet kept them back from the end. There was a lot of fanfare from them. Then the barker got going.

"Ladeez and gents! The Great Mordini will now give an exhibition of fearlessness which is unsurpassed in this civ-il-ized worrld! He will be sealed in a coffin and lowered down into the murrky depths of the sea, to remain there without air for the next three hours. Death-defying, ladeez and gents! Death-defying!..."

Bill Hanley

I looked at the Harlem River. It looked mighty cold and grim. I didn't envy Mordini. I called to a dock hand: "Hey, Cholly, how deep is it off this end?"

The dock hand stared at me doubtfully and scratched his chin. "Well," he said, "at high tide it's about twenty feet, but it's low tide now and I don't reckon it's over fifteen right straight down where the coffin'll go."

"Maybe we can see it on the bottom," Hanley said.

I chortled: "Through that muck?" and pointed at the Harlem, which is no sparkling burgundy as you know. It's thick with dirt and you can't see two feet beneath the surface. "You know," I went on, "if it's low tide, then the other end of this dock is out of water. I mean where the pilings go down into the mud, there's dry land when it's low tide."

"How can you tell?"

"Stands to reason. Take a look there. The water doesn't come up to the middle piling. It's dry below. There must be a sudden drop right close to the end of the pier. That makes it deeper right here."

The man with the blowtorch pulled the canvas away. We saw the coffin. It was painted a dull gray, a queer kind of color, and it had a single hooked V at the head where the lowering tackle would attach itself. They lifted the cover off. The inside was very plain, just a couple of comfortable cushions on the floor and a pillow for his head.

I got over to Mordini and stood by him as he took off his shoes and climbed into the coffin. "Mordini! Mordini!" I yelled above the racket. "I'm a reporter! What are your last words?"

Flat on his back, his mouth split into a sickly grin, he said: "I'll see you at two o'clock."

"That's a helluva epitaph," I said dourly.

"The hand is quicker than the eye, buddy," he said. "I'll be seeing you."

"I wouldn't bet on it," I muttered as they placed the lid on the coffin.

Hanley nudged me. "He seems sure of himself."

I nodded. "Yeah. Too sure. Especially with the five fish I bet against it. What's his take on this?"

"No take," said Hanley. "It's a free show absolutely."

"Listen," I replied, "he's making a take somewhere. He isn't going down there for his health and to give the people of this fair city a good time in case his corpse rises at two o'clock. This whole thing is on the queer. I don't figure it."

"My, my," Hanley laughed. "So Daffy Dill is sleuthing again."

"Ertsnay," I snapped and watched the man with the blowtorch go to work. From the can he took out something that was hard as the devil and looked gummy. He lighted the blowtorch and set the flame on the gum and pretty soon the gum began to melt.

He held the wad in a pair of tongs over the lid of the coffin. The melted gum ran down and into the crack of the lid and there it hardened almost immediately. The guy did this all around the seam until the whole lid was hermetically sealed like a can of spinach.

"And now, ladeez and gents," roared the barker, while the dock hands swung the coffin around and fixed the hook to the tackle to lower it down, "Mordini will attempt to show you how the famous Hindu yogis can remain buried underground for days! Let 'er go, boys!"

They swung the coffin out and slowly began to lower it into the water. The man with the torch said: "If you see bubbles, pull it right out. That'll mean it isn't fully sealed."

But there were no bubbles. That grave box was sealed all right. And while no water could get in, no air could get in either, and I didn't have to be a scientist to know that there wasn't enough air in a coffin to keep a man alive for three hours.

The coffin was in the water, then the head went under. I could see it go down about a foot and finally it disappeared completely in the muck of the river. They kept lowering on the tackle until the coffin hit the bottom and the line slackened. Then they stopped. Mordini was on the bottom, a pillow under his head and the Harlem River on his chest.

As soon as all was clear and the crowd sat down morbidly to wait for the passage of the three hours in hope of seeing a particularly gorgeous cadaver, the man with the torch nodded to the barker and disappeared in the crowd. I had a hunch he was lamming too early in the thing, but I couldn't keep my eye on him and I lost him.

"I bet it's cold down there," Hanley said, shivering.

"Don't get sentimental," I said.

I stuck around there for half an hour before I suddenly

realized that I had another assignment to go over and revel in the warm sunshine of Sylvia Calmette's smile and to kiss the lily white hand which brought the chink of coppers into the paybox of the lucky cinema palace which happened to have one of her pictures showing.

I shrugged, took one last look at the muddy surface of the river. "Well," I said, "that's one way to die." And I started off.

"Where you going?" Hanley asked.

"To heaven, you big bold policeman!"

3

AS ITEMIZED PREVIOUSLY, the Superlative New York studios were a mere four blocks away from the scene of the coffin wash and I dragged my reluctant toes along the way until I reached the main entrance of the place, which had a big sign: *Superlative Pictures, Inc.*, on the door and which, cannily, I avoided.

I went around the side alley and reached the door where they let in the extras every time they wanted a mob scene or the faded glory of Caesar's armies and I found a big burly cop there, swinging a nightstick and regarding me with a glance which was plainly carbolic. Undaunted, I pranced up to him, gave him my best disarming grin and showed him my press card and said: "Gentleman of the press, officer."

He nodded me through, which is unusual, for I generally have the skin they love to clutch.

Once inside the big sound-proof door I was grabbed by a yes-man who pointed at a *Silence* sign and whispered raucously in my left ear: "They're shooting a scene over there. Keep quiet or you'll ruin the take. Who you want to see?"

"The heart throb of a million men," I said. "Where is she?"

"She's on the set. She's in the scene. It's Cleopatra's death where she stings herself with a garter snake. Shh. You can go over and watch if you want to, but don't breathe. Shh."

I went over to where the Kleig lights made a brighter than daylight splotch upon a huge set with ornate draperies and a papier-mâché marble throne on which—oh, pangs of delight—the winsome, pulchritudinous Sylvia Calmette reposed, garbed in little or nothing like the queen of the ancient Egyptians. I caught onto the action about then and realized that she had just allowed the asp (garter-snake) to bite her and that she was now in the throes of death.

She did a pretty good job, but I thought she'd never get through dying. And then a sharp-voiced director yipped: "Cut!" and every stage hand and mechanic in the place applauded her loudly.

She sighed prettily and acknowledged the triumph in a way that showed she was modest and shy and she tried to blush but couldn't.

I pushed through the mob and tried to get close to her, but the nearest I could do was tail her to her room, which presently led away from the twitter-twatter and down a quiet corridor to a door with the words: *Sylvia Calmette* on it, large enough for a frog on the Eiffel Tower to make out.

I had a sort of hunch then and I stayed behind her a little, realizing that I could get a better interview in her dressing room than by shooting embarrassing questions in the corridor, and, besides, I wanted her to lose the maid, which same, was a peculiar looking specimen with a nose like a ruler and a chin like the rock of Gibraltar. Sylvia reached her door and opened it. Then she gasped and I heard distinctly a male voice snap: "Send her away and keep quiet...."

She turned to the maid and said: "I'll call you when I need you."

AS SOON AS the maid had gone, Sylvia opened the door hurriedly and slipped in, closing it behind her. I stole up to it then and heard the lock click. Glancing around and feeling like peeping tommy, I made sure no traffic was passing. The corridor was deserted, apparently, and *tabu* to other employees, this kind thought being to let the star rest in peace between shooting of the scenes.

I plastered my ear against the door and listened. For a minute there wasn't a sound and I had the feeling that the bird in there with her was listening at the door too. Then I heard his short footsteps go across the room and Sylvia Calmette snapped: "You've got a helluva nerve, busting in here like this! I thought you were supposed to be—"

"Cut that," the man growled. "Keep your mouth shut!"

While my illusions about the sweet and simple Sylvia went flying out of the rear alley at the old-fashioned way she reeled out the ole epithet, I had a funny feeling. The man's voice was familiar. I'd heard it somewhere before.

"Say," she shot back at him, "what is this? Who do you think you are, anyway? I told you not to come around the studio! When I want you around I tell you so. Otherwise, steer clear."

The man said nastily: "Don't give me that."

"Oh, no?" she said, just as nastily. "Feeling your weight pretty much, aren't you? Listen, you cheap grafter, maybe you'd like me to get loose-tongued. Maybe you'd like to go a stretch at San Quentin or hit the end of a rope."

"I've been thinking about that for the last year," he said evenly, and in tones that began to give me the shivers.

He sounded cold as ice and he meant business. "All right, Sylvia, you saw me and your word could get me extradited back to California, and maybe hung in the bargain."

"You know damn well it would!"

"For the last year," the man went on, "ever since that night when Duncan was—when Duncan shot himself—"

She laughed harshly. "That's hot—shot himself!"

"Since that night," the man said, ignoring her stab, "I've let you blackmail me for every cent I've had. I had to. I had to follow you around wherever you went, do what you told me to do, become such a close companion that everybody got an idea there was something between us. Well, now I'm broke and I'm no good to you. Why do you hang on to me?"

She laughed again. "I'm no fool, Harry. Your old man may have disowned you, but he's still got a couple of million dollars in his jeans. And it just might happen that some day, when he kicks the bucket, he may get senile and soft-brained and leave it to you. And if he does—I want to have you around—in case I get ideas of marriage. Yeah, you heard me. I'd even marry *you* for a couple of million."

"I figured you that way. Sylvia, you're nothing but a cheap, dirty little rat. I once told you I could stand so much and no more. I'm telling you again."

She sneered: "And what are you going to do?"

"You're the only witness to that Duncan affair," he replied. "You're the only one who could send me back to face that murder charge. Haven't you ever wondered that I might—kill you?"

"Sure." She laughed nervously.

"But you haven't the nerve."

"I had the nerve to kill Duncan."

"Sure, but you wouldn't try it again. If anything happened to me, Harry, there'd be an investigation. And if I was murdered you'd be dragged up as the logical killer, because I'm supposed to be your mistress. And if they didn't get you on my count, they'd sure drag up the Duncan affair again, and remember that they never closed that case and that you figured pretty prominently in it. You wouldn't kill me, Harry," she finished sneeringly. "Not unless you had a perfect alibi, and you're not smart enough to get a perfect alibi."

I HAD A story right here and I was letting it get away from me. I swore softly under my breath and dropped to my knees, peeking through the keyhole to get a look at the poor sucker who'd been playing Poppa to America's sex appeal for the last year. I couldn't see anything through the keyhole but an unoccupied chaise-longue.

I got to my feet. I rapped on the door. There was a heavy silence.

She called: "Who is it?"

"Daffy Dill," I said, "of the New York *Chronicle.*"

Her voice softened instantly and she replied sweetly: "Oh, Mr. Dill, what is it you want?"

"An interview for your adoring public," I replied.

There were hasty whispers.

"Just a mo-ment," she called. There were scuffles and I waited a good half minute before the lock clicked and she let me in. Close to, she was really a stunner. I nearly forgot that Dinah Mason was the gal I was carrying the torch for. But I could see a hardness in Sylvia's face that didn't appeal to me.

I looked around as she closed the door and wondered

where in hell the man had gone. I saw a closet door opened a notch.

She smiled disarmingly. "You said you wanted an interview, Mr. Drill?"

"Dill's the name," I said. "Yes."

She stretched out on the chaise-longue and lighted a cigarette. "Very well," she smiled. "And what would you like to know?"

"First," I asked, "just what is your reaction to the Great Mordini's underwater experiment in the coffin, now going on?"

Her face went white and she sat up as though I had hit her. She threw the cigarette into a tray and snapped a glance at the closet door. She gasped too genuinely; then when she saw me eye her with suspicion, she gasped again—like Cleopatra would have—and made a pretty hammy swoon back on the chaise-longue.

I sighed. "What's the matter?"

"I feel... so... faint," she whispered, imitating the imitators of Sara Bernhardt poorly. "Would you mind... getting me a glass of water?"

It was my cue for an exit and I decided to play along. "Sure," I said. "I'll be back in a minute. Where do I get it?"

"Over by the movie set," she answered, giving me the longest route in the building and failing to realize that she had a pair of nice nickel faucets in her own room. But who was I to argue?

I closed the door behind me firmly and made much noise like galloping horses down the corridor. I crept right back to the door then and stood there, waiting for the guy inside to come out in his flight so's I could get a look at him.

I took out a cigarette, expecting him to leave almost immediately. I was just lighting it when there was a sharp crack in Sylvia Calmette's room, followed nearly simultaneously by a wheezing cough and then the thud of a falling body.

I dropped the cigarette and match in pure astonishment and turned to open the door when the knob fell back away from me and *I came face to face with Mordini, who was in a sealed coffin under the Harlem River!*

IN HIS LEFT hand he carried a smoking automatic pistol, a big son of a gun that I took for a forty-five.

And over his shoulder on the floor with a hole through the middle of her pretty face lay Cleopatra, her scanty silks all awry, but her short black wig sturdily in place despite the slug that had passed through the back of it.

I was so stunned for the second that I couldn't move.

Mordini stared at me in blind fury, just as stunned.

Then I gave a hoarse futile bellow and lunged toward him, but he had collected himself faster than I did and he raised the gun. I thought I was a goner at that range and I knew that if he pulled the trigger the brains behind the year's best scoops would be ignomininously spattered over the floor of the Superlative Pictures, Inc., studio.

But he didn't shoot me. When I saw the raised gun I pulled up indecisively. That gave him the margin of time he needed. He reversed the gun, turning down the big stock and gripping the barrel in his paw.

Instantly I caught what he planned to do. I let go one of my prize hooks in the general direction of his invisible jaw.

I missed.

The blow, with the impetus behind it, pulled me forward

off my feet just as he cracked me squarely between the eyes with the end of the gun.

As I went down, I saw only one thing through the black curtain that was coming down over my eyes.

It was the huddled form of Sylvia Calmette, dead not ten feet from where I hit.

And the asp that had bitten her—was a forty-five slug.

Then I went out—like prosperity....

4

THE FIRST THING I saw when I came to was the sad-faced yes-man who had spoken to me when I first came in. He was asking me if I was all right.

"Lemme up," I said. My head ached like hell.

"Did you kill her?" he asked, helping me up.

"Me kill her?" I snapped. "And tell me who laid this egg on my skull—a Rhode Island Red?"

"You didn't bump her?"

"No, for God's sake! What time is it?"

"It's twenty of two," he said.

"Call the cops," I said. "I've got to go somewhere. I'll be back. Tell Inspector Halloran that I'll be back with Bill Hanley!"

"Sure," he said, wide-eyed. "Sure I will."

I went out the alley door like a whirlwind. I did those four blocks to Pier 64 in better time than Nurmi could have made. When I pulled up on the dock the crowd was on its feet and waiting expectantly around the end of the pier.

I was panting like an angel fish as I forced my way through the mob to the end of the pier. Bill Hanley saw me and grinned.

He said: "Now, Daffy, don't tell me it was the spoon in your coffee that put that bump on your head. How many times have I told you that most of the gals you whistle at have husbands?"

"Bill," I said, "so help me, listen. Sylvia Calmette's been murdered!"

He stared at me. "What?"

"She's been shot and killed! And I was right outside her door when the gunner came out. He ran into me and slugged me with the rod! I saw him!"

"When was this?" Hanley asked in a low voice.

"About twelve. He clonked me down and out for an hour and a half. When I came to it was just after one-thirty, so I beat it down here to tell you because—"

"You saw the guy?"

"Yeah."

"Know him?"

"You bet your sweet life I know him!" I exclaimed. "It was the Great Mordini, Bill, in all his viperine glory."

Hanley gasped and stared at the river. "But he's down there, Daffy! I'll swear he is! They haven't lifted the coffin yet!"

"But he won't be in it when they do," I said. "Don't worry about that. I tell you I saw him. He wasn't one foot from me and I know it was Mordini! He killed her because she was blackmailing him!"

"On what account?"

"I'm not sure," I said. "I'll have to look that up."

"It's two," said Hanley. "Here comes the barker. The coffin'll be up in a minute. Let's wait."

We waited. The dock hands got the signal from the barker and they strained on the tackle. The line snapped taut and slowly began to lift the aluminum coffin from the bottom while the barker gave us a swell spiel again.

THE COFFIN BROKE through the surface and rose up to the level of the dock. They swung it in and laid it down flat on the boards. Every one crowded around close. Then the fellow with the blowtorch appeared again, just as mysteriously as he had disappeared. His trousers were caked with mud, and I wondered where in hell he'd been. He got to work on the sealing gum with the flame and melted it into liquid. When it was soft, the dock hands grabbed the cover of the coffin and lifted it off.

There—on the cushions and the pillow—lay Mordini!

He grinned weakly and slowly got up to his feet. The crowd went wild, and I felt like a fool. Hanley stared at him too and then at me. Mordini caught my eye in a faint flicker of recognition, and I knew I was right on the whole business. The little runt had killed Cleopatra and had slugged me too.

But how?

I knew damn well I couldn't go to Halloran and tell him that Mordini was the killer. The alibi was too good. How could a man be sealed in a coffin, lowered under a river, get out of it, go to a studio four blocks away, shoot a woman, and get back into the coffin?

Until I figured that one out I was out in the rain without an umbrella.

Mordini put on the shoes he had left on the dock, and after a short speech he started away. Hanley looked dubious. "Well, Daffy," he said, "I can't very well arrest that bird. He couldn't have done it. Are you sure?"

I said: "Dead sure, Bill, but he's put one over. I'm going

downtown. Just get the name and address of the guy with the blowtorch and I'll see you later."

"O.K.," Hanley said.

I caught a cab and gave the driver the address of the *Chronicle.* It took a good half hour to make the building, and I breezed in without so much as a nod to Dinah, who took the rebuke stoically. I went into the newspaper morgue and grabbed Old Hank Benton, who handles it.

"What is it, Daffy?" he asked.

"Ever hear of a guy named Duncan?" I asked. "Hollywood is the locale and he died approximately a year ago."

"I'll see," Hank said and disappeared among the rows of steel files. He was back in two minutes flat and he had a portfolio in his hands which gladdened my heart. "Here's your meat," he said.

I took the portfolio and sat down and went through it. The dead man was Charles Duncan, a famous director for Superlative Pictures, who had "committed suicide" after a dinner party. I'd never heard of the bird, which is not unusual. He had been in love with Sylvia Calmette and supposedly killed himself because she did not return the affection. Held at the first investigation on a possible charge of homicide was a man named Harry Wordell, who was later released, due to lack of evidence.

"Hank," I said, "get me a portfolio on a bird named Harry Wordell."

I looked through the rest of the copy on the Duncan "suicide," and I had hardly finished when Benton came back with a second portfolio. I opened it and went through it. Harry Wordell, from the newspaper stories, was the scion of a wealthy Chicago family, son of Egbert Wordell, the millionaire. Senior Wordell had disowned Harry when the boy went to Hollywood to become an actor. Harry had met up with a famous escape artist and magician in Hollywood, and after the Duncan smell he had changed his name to Harry Mordini, the Great Mordini, and toured the country, showing all he had learned in magic and contortion.

THEN THE WHOLE thing was as plain as Bill Hanley's face. Mordini was my man all right. But how he had worked the trick was a mystery!

"Thanks, Hank," I said. I gave him the stuff and breezed into the city room. I yipped the story to a rewrite man, and when I had finished I went out of there like a light and back uptown to the Superlative studios.

Bill Hanley was waiting for me in front of the place. "Halloran told me to tell you that you're nuttier than ever. He admits that Mordini would be a swell and logical catch to the affair, but he wishes you would explain just how he was able to be under the Harlem river and in Sylvia Calmette's room at the same time."

"Hell with him," I growled, annoyed. "I thought there might be twins. You know, one goes down while the other kills, but that didn't work out. Mordini is Harry Wordell of Chicago, and he is no twin. I've got an idea though. The guy with the blowtorch knows something, Bill. He scrammed right after the coffin went down, and when he got back, just in time to open the thing, there was mud on his pants. Let's see him and make him talk."

"O.K. by me," said Hanley. "He's Dan Garrel, 445 E. 178th St., Bronx."

We hopped another hack and I marveled at the free and

easy manner in which I was spending the *Chronicle's* money. We made the trip across the bridge and into the Bronx in something under nothing flat.

We went up the stairs of a big ordinary apartment house just off the Grand Concourse, to the third floor. There was a door with Garrel's name on it. We rang the bell.

No answer.

We rang it again. Still no answer.

Hanley tried the knob. The door opened.

We went in.

We didn't have to go very far either. Right after we came through the small foyer to the living room we found Dan Garrel—the man with the blowtorch—dead in his own blood on the floor.

A forty-five slug had plugged through the middle of his face. His eyes and his nose were a mess. And the back of his thick skull, where the lead had exited, was no pageant of roses itself!

"Hey, derp," Hanley growled. "Lookit that!" He whistled as he pointed his finger. I lamped a fifty spot bill, brand new, in Garrel's dead right hand.

We didn't say anything for several seconds. We just sort of looked around, feeling badly. Then I asked: "Surprised, Poppa?"

"No," Hanley said quickly. "I ain't surprised at all. Mordini's my man all right. The lay is as plain as day. This egg helped Mordini pull the trick. And he had to be killed to cover Mordini's tracks. And that's the fifty spot Mordini paid him—probably just as he bumped the poor guy."

"You should be promoted, Hanley," I said dryly. "You get smarter all the time."

"Yeah," Hanley sighed. "I get so smart that it's just my luck to have the perfect murder dumped right into my lap."

I said: "Perfect murder?"

"What else, Daffy?" Hanley threw up his hands in despair. "What do you expect me to do? First—the Cleopatra dame. Then Garrel. I can tie both of them right around Mordini's neck. It would be a circumstantial net that only a miracle could break. Then Mordini would spring his miracle and break it! That's the hell of the thing! Mordini was in a casket under a river when Calmette was shot. God knows where he was when he killed Garrel, but I bet his alibi is a honey for that too. It's perfect, Daffy!"

"It's a trick," I said.

"Sure, sure," said Hanley. "A trick. What else could it be? Somehow, he got out of the coffin and played murder. Somehow he got back into it again safe and sound. Somehow, although there was a wet river on top of the coffin, the inside is as dry as Inspector Halloran's dirty cracks. A trick! Sure, it's a trick! But it's a trick I'll never be able to figure out. He's an escape artist, Daffy. It might have taken him a couple of years to work the thing out. There was only one guy who could have known what the trick was. And that guy is Garrel—and he's gonna be a big help, I don't think!"

"So be it," I said, noticing the time. "It's your worry, not mine. When you make the arrest you can count on me to identify him as the bird who laid a beaut on my skull when he dashed out of Cleopatra's dressing room."

Hanley groaned: "Where's a telephone?"

I HANDED IT to him. He called the bureau and asked for Doc Kyne, chief M.E., and a Public Welfare car to transport the corpse to the morgue.

When he was finished I called the *Chronicle* and spilled the story.

When I finished I found Hanley had grabbed a chair and was looking mighty sad. Plainly, he'd given the thing up.

I waved to him and started for the door. "I'll call you at h.q. if anything new breaks."

Hanley asked: "What you gonna do?"

"Think," I said.

"I was afraid of that," he muttered. "So it's still the perfect murder as far as I'm concerned."

I left the apartment and went out front. I was just going to catch a cab when I got an idea. I turned back and went down the stairs in front of the house to the superintendent. He lived in the basement and he turned out to be a harmless old Swede with a frowsy mop on his upper lip. I said: "Know a guy named Garrel, friend?"

"Sure," he said. "I bane know him. Dan Garrel. Third floor front of the house."

"Know what he does for a living?"

"Sure, sure. He iss a salvitch diver."

I ogled, my Swedish not being so hot. "A what?"

"A salvitch diver. He does down under the water, bane looking for gold and shipwrecks. Smart man. He makes money plenty."

"A salvage diver!" I exclaimed. "Eureka!"

This time the Swede ogled. "What iss that eureka stuff?"

"That, my pal," I said jubilantly, "is merely a good ole American expression, which means that in the end Justice Will Prevail for the Righteous. Thanks!" And I lammed.

In the chartered hack—on my way to East 86th and Park

Avenue, where the Great Mordini, alias Harry Wordell, was located in the Wanderwell Hotel, one of the city's better stys—hunches and hunches piled up on me. I had a clue, by God, and I would work it rugged until it couldn't stand up under its own strength any more.

5

MORDINI WAS A cool one. I had to give him credit for that. When I rang the bell to his suite on the eighth floor he opened the door nonchalantly and stared at me.

"Hello," I said.

He smiled peculiarly. "Come in," he said.

He locked the door behind me. Then he crossed the room to an easy chair and sat down and lighted a cigarette.

He said: "Well?"

I shook my head. "Am I nerts, or do you really recognize me?"

"You're the reporter," he said, smiling. "The one who thought I was committing suicide this afternoon."

"Is that all you remember?"

He shrugged. "What the hell, Dill, I'm sorry about your skull. I was in a hurry and you got in my way. What else could I do?"

"You could have honked your horn," I said.

"Hurt bad?"

"I was out for an hour and a half," I said, "and I had a bump like the spine of a whale." I paused, frowning. "I don't get you, Mordini. Are you admitting that you were in Sylvia Calmette's room this afternoon?"

He smiled thinly. "You saw me, didn't you?"

I gaped. "You admit it?"

"Sure. To *you.*" He blew out a ring of smoke through his nose. "What can I lose?"

I nodded again. "I get it. For a moment I thought you were breaking down and confessing. You shot her all right, didn't you?"

"Sure. If you listened you know why, too."

I was beginning to like the little son of a gun. If it hadn't been for the fact that I liked Bill Hanley far more and that the case would be a black mark on Hanley's record if it went unsolved I might have had a drink with Mordini and forgotten the whole thing.

"Listen, Dill," he told me in a low voice. "I don't mind telling you. My alibi is perfect, unbreakable. It took brains to think it up. It took two years of planning. And then it took a helluva lot of nerve to go through with it. You can pin all the motives and other dope you want onto me. But you can't make a jury believe I wasn't in that casket under that river. And if some expert—like yourself—should figure it out on paper a jury wouldn't believe it, see?"

"I see," I said. "But if selfsame expert not only showed it on paper, but also went through with the trick—I guess that would convince a jury that it could be done."

"Thinking of trying it?"

"Kind of."

He laughed heartily and got up and slapped me on the back. "I like you," he said. "But I flatter myself with that trick. Go ahead, Dill, and try it, and after it's over send your bulls to arrest me—if you're still alive. Of course, I can't say where I'll be in 1938. That's three years from now."

He began to annoy me with his damned gloating. I gave

him a stab. "Three years, eh? Well, I dunno. It might take me that long to find another diver like Dan Garrel."

THAT HIT HIM. He took the cig' from his mouth and stared at me. "What did you say?"

"Dan Garrel," I said. "You know. The guy who used to blowtorch to open you up. The guy who put the sealing wax on your coffin."

"What—about him?" Mordini asked slowly.

"Somebody shot him," I answered. "Probably the same gun that killed Cleopatra. The cops can tell from the markings of the slugs. He was a diver, pal, didn't you know?"

"No," said Mordini coldly. "You know, Dill, you're a dangerous newsy to have around. If I were the guy who killed Garrel I'd sort of try to put you out of the way."

"I figured that," I said. "It's this way. I think there's enough rope and dope around the killer of Calmette and Garrel so that one little thing might get a guilty verdict—without proving that the casket escape was a trick."

Mordini's eyes were ice.

"I don't get you," he said.

"Suppose," I said, "that I found the rod that killed both of them on you..." I watched his eyes jump away from me for a moment and then come back.

He said: "Yeah?"

"In that case I could prove that even if you were in the casket during Cleopatra's bumping off you had the gun that did it and therefore must be either the killer himself or an accessory *before* the fact. That—along with the fact that the beautiful Sylvia saw you kill Charles Duncan, the Hollywood director, because you were jealous of the way he was cutting you out with her—would fix your wagon.

Sylvia sank her fangs into you, especially after she learned your moniker was Wordell and that your old man might leave you a couple of millions some day. She had you. You hated her. So plunko. Dead Cleopatra tells no tales. No, Mordini. All that wouldn't help you a bit."

"I believe you," Mordini purred, smiling again in an oily way. "But you'd have to find the gun to make all that stick, wouldn't you?"

"Yep," I said.

He sighed. "What a pity. The barrel is somewhere in the Hudson River. The magazine is somewhere in the East River. The stock of the rod is somewhere in the Harlem River."

"Thought so," I lied, grinning. "That's a hot joke on the three dicks who are shadowing you."

"What?"

"Sure," I went on lying. "They can't arrest you, but they suspect you. They have orders to tail you wherever you go and to frisk you for the rod. They also have the hotel help fixed so that you can't send the gun out in parcels or anything. Mordini, if you hadn't gotten rid of that gun today and if you had tried to leave this place with it you'd have been a first-class candidate for the chair."

"Yeah..." he said absently.

He sounded as though he were thinking hard about something. I got up.

"Toodle-oo," I said. "I'll have to catch you the hard way—by duplicating your casket escape."

"You do that little thing," he said.

"Thanks for coming."

"Not at all, not at all," I said. The door closed after me.

I went to the elevator, feeling pretty good. One thing I knew—the rod that killed Sylvia Calmette was still in Mordini's apartment. It was impossible for him to have shot Carrel with it at four o'clock and then to have dissembled the thing and thrown the three parts into three different rivers and still have been in his room when I got there.

And my neat little lies had scared him. It was a sure thing that he wouldn't try to smuggle the gun out of the Wanderwell. He had too much to lose at this point, and taking chances wasn't worth while.

I WENT HOME and drank a trio of Stingers for supper. Then I got some paper and pencil and went to work. I felt like Thurston. I worked on that paper, making plans, destroying them, making them again, and on into the night.

Around nine o'clock I hit it. I'd been stumped the whole time until I remembered that the tide in the Harlem had been at full low when Mordini did the thing. And that struck me in the eyes. Recalling what the old-timer had told me about depth when I asked him on the pier that morning, I drew me a sketch. When the sketch was finished I had another Stinger to celebrate my genius. Then I called headquarters.

I got grizzled old Inspector Halloran himself and he sounded like four fighting mountain lions, he was that mad.

"Professor," I said, "I have solved the mystery of Sylvia Calmette's murder, to say nothing of Carrel's too. Is Hanley there?"

"He's here, Daffy," Halloran roared. "But, by God, you're telling me—not him. Who did it?"

"Mordini," I said.

"I *know* Mordini done it! That part's easy! But how did he do it? That's the point! Did you find out how he did it?"

"I did," I said.

"How?"

"Since I know," I said, "this is one time, Inspector, that you take your orders from me."

"All right, all right," Halloran grated, grinding his teeth savagely into the mouthpiece. "I'll play games with you—only tell me how he did it!"

"Then, listen. At eleven-thirty A.M. tomorrow, one Daffy Dill is going to go down in a casket and remain under water for three hours—yea, verily, even as the Great Mordini did it. Furthermore, to add weight to public opinion on the Law's side of the case, the *Chronicle* will headline the event and generally draw a crowd. Then and then alone I'll show how he did it. I'll do it myself!"

"You will?" Halloran sounded almost respectful. "Daffy—your idea is the nuts and just the ballyhoo we need to put the thing over. But can you do it?"

"If I can't," I said, "make it a nice funeral."

"Anything else?"

"Yes. I want Hanley and another dick to pick up Mordini and bring him along to watch the show. Make sure of that or he may skip when he hears about it. Right?"

"Right!" Halloran exclaimed. "And where does the show come off?"

"Pier 64 on the Harlem River," I said. "And now—since this may be my last night on earth—I am going to retire and I warn you right now that there's no sense in phoning me back. I'll only turn over in my bed and say: 'The hell with Halloran.' G'night, Toots."

I hung up. I waited a second or two and then I called the Old Man at his home and got him half-hysterical with excitement. I gave him the whole yarn, and when I finally put down the hand set he was raving something about headlines, handling it himself, and me being a general damn fool all around.

The last thing I did with the telephone was to call the Universal Salvaging Company. They promised to send over a diver, one Thomas Burkes, early in the morning.

6

TOMMY BURKES AND I arrived at Pier 64 at exactly eleven o'clock the next morning. This Burkes was a giant with hands like Carnera's and a flashy mind like Baer's. He was smart and no mistake, and it hadn't taken me long to get him into the spirit of the thing when I explained it to him at my spot.

Burkes and I pushed through the crowd until we reached the end of the pier. Hanley was there, worried. Halloran was there, barking but not biting. A cordon of cops held the mob back. The Old Man was there, superintending the primary testing of the casket to make sure it didn't leak. Mordini was there. Why not? It was his casket. Hanley had seen to a borrow of the thing which Mordini—diplomatically—had to agree to. There were two dicks on either side of him when I passed him. He said:

"Dill—you're crazy to try it."

"You lived," I said, and he shrugged.

I passed him and reached the Old Man.

I said, "The casket all ready, boss?"

"All ready," said the Old Man soberly. "By God, Daffy, I hope you know what you're doing. I like a scoop as well as anybody, but it isn't my desire to read your obit."

"That crack'll cost you a raise," I said.

Inspector Halloran nudged my arm. "O.K.," I told him.

"I'm all set to go. One thing. This guy, his name is Tommy Burkes, seals the coffin, get it? He and he alone. Now I'm doing a repeat of the Mordini act. I'm going down now and I'll stay down until two o'clock. While I'm down there I'll run around the city and have a good time. And I'll bring you back proof that I was out of the coffin while you thought I was in it. Search me."

Hanley and Inspector Halloran went to it and frisked me up and down as though I were a dip. Hanley said: "You're carrying nothing but a fake mustache and three bucks."

"Good," I said. "Give me them back. I go into this coffin with three bucks and a mustache. I'll come out with the home edition of the *Chronicle,* which hasn't been published yet, and for an extra little gift I'll bring you the rod that killed Sylvia Calmette and Dan Garrel."

"What?" Inspector Halloran bellowed.

"Sure," I said. I waved to Mordini. "Did you hear that? I'm going to come up with the rod that fired the slug for Cleopatra."

Mordini jumped, startled, and went white as a ghost.

I waved to them all and lay down in the aluminum casket. Bill Hanley leaned down over me. "You all right, Daffy?"

"Right," I whispered. "Bill—one thing can slip me up. Mordini. Do me a personal favor. Put the bracelets on him and chain one end to yourself. Otherwise—"

Hanley nodded, his jaw stiffening. "Consider it done, pal."

"Then lower away."

THE NEXT THING I knew, the lid of the casket was on and

there I reposed in blackness. It was thick blackness too, and it scared the pants off me at first. I started to get panicky and breathe heavily. Somehow I stopped that. I stopped the queer sickness in the pit of my stomach too. There were dull sounds outside the coffin, but no human voices. It was a pretty rotten sort of a situation, all in all.

It seemed a long time, waiting, and I was beginning to think the air might give out before time. Suddenly the casket moved. It kept moving too. It slid along the dock and then yawed into space, the bottom dropping away with suddenness which made me gasp, casket moved. It kept moving, too. It began to lower. I could feel the jerks of the tow-line.

I held one hand against the aluminum lid. It was tough going, doing this, because there wasn't much elbow room in the metal kimona, but I wanted to check. In a second or two, the aluminum went cold as ice. I was under the river's surface. Anxiously, I held my breath and waited to see if the water might find some little crevice which the sealing wax had overlooked.

It didn't. The casket was airtight.

Far be it from a Dill to exaggerate, but it took exactly ninety-nine years for that casket to go down twenty feet to the bottom of the Harlem, where it hit, bottom first, and then slowly fell back so that I was lying face up.

Up above, the show was over. To the spectators, I was down until two o'clock. Lying there, I got the jitters thinking about that much of a wait. Already the air was getting thick and breathing was being made difficult. I breathed shallowly and hung on, waiting for Tommy Burkes to make good or else.

He made good. The casket began to move. Not up either. It was being hauled along the river bottom. This went on for a long time. He must have had a pretty tough job. It hit an incline, leaving my head way below my feet and not making me any more comfortable. Presently I stopped moving. There was a new sound, a metallic scraping as of a chisel along the seams of the aluminum lid. Fresh air poured into the casket. It felt like a stiff drink and I drank it thankfully. A voice said: "Heave!"

I heaved against the lid and it went up. Tommy Burkes stood over me and lifted it off. "All right, lad?" he asked.

"Ducky," I said. "How's the ground?"

"Dry enough," he replied. "You can git out."

I climbed out into the promised land and stretched. Burkes looked queer in his big rubber diving suit. Beside the casket on the mud was a huge steel head with a single glass eye—his diving helmet.

Over us, thudding with the beat of many feet, was Pier 64, Harlem River, from which I had been lowered. We were underneath it and dry as a bone, and it had been pretty simple at that.

Here's what happened. Burkes sealed my casket up before I was lowered down. As soon as he had finished he left the crowd on the pier and crawled down underneath it. Now Mordini's big punch lay in the fact that the river had to be at *low tide* when the trick was pulled. I had figured that when it was at low tide there was a space under the pier which went dry as the waters receded. It was right. At low tide a good ten foot area was left high and dry.

So Burkes came down there, donned his diving outfit, and then hiked down into the river after me. He found my casket where it had hit. He'd unhooked it from the tackle, and then dragged it back under the pier to the dry space, where he chiselled the sealing wax off and let me out. Simple, eh wot?

OF COURSE THE aluminum casket itself was light as a feather. It was only my own weight which kept it from floating when it was lowered under water. So Burkes hadn't had much weight to pull out of the water onto the muddy beach under the pier. He'd had only my own weight.

"Well, friend," I said, fixing the fake mustache on my upper lip, "I'm off to the wars. I'll be back at a quarter of two for my rebirth."

"Shure," grinned Burkes. "I think I'll eat now myself."

I left him and crawled up from beneath the dock and mingled with the crowd. Then I hit east down the block.

I grabbed a sandwich in the Automat and then rode a larruping hack down to 86th to the Wanderwell Hotel. It was twelve-thirty when I finally got there.

I rode the elevator to the eighth floor and ambled out. Thence to Mordini's quarters, which same I opened very easily with a skeleton key from the bunch on my key ring. I went in and closed the door.

For fifteen minutes I searched. Tore the joint wide open, but found no sign of that forty-five that Mordini had used to bump Calmette and Carrel. And it had to be there. I knew he couldn't have taken it out.

I craned my neck to survey the side of the hotel building around the window. Nothing there.

I closed the right window and opened the left.

I glanced up. Son of a gun! That little runt Mordini had taken the forty-five all intact and he had plastered it up on the side of the hotel wall, eight floors above the street, with four thick pieces of adhesive tape!

I nearly floored myself on 86th Street trying to get it down.

That ended it. I bought a home edition of the *Chronicle* and took good time getting back to Pier 64. I climbed down under it and met Burkes, waiting for me. At a quarter of two I got in the casket with the paper and the gun. He sealed me up, put on his helmet and dragged me back under the river, where he hooked the line to the casket again. Promptly at two I was hoisted up, and when they took off the lid there I was with Mordini's rod in my hand.

Mordini took it well. He turned a little white at first, but when Bill Hanley arrested him for Calmette's murder he just shrugged and smiled at me and said: "I guess you win, Dill."

"Not only from you," I said, "but from Poppa too."

Hanley frowned. "From me? How come?"

"Five fish," I said. "When Mordini made his dive you bet me five fish that he'd stay under the whole three hours. If he *had* stayed under you couldn't arrest him because he couldn't have killed Cleopatra. So by arresting him you lose the bet."

He forked out. "Well, you can't always win," he grumbled. "I made the pinch, anyhow."

That night—on the new-found wealth—Dinah and I got completely ossified. That week—through the solving of the Calmette case—Hanley got promoted to a lieutenant's berth.

And that month—by the skin of his teeth—Mordini, alias Harry Wordell, was lucky enough to get life....

ABOUT THE AUTHOR

I WAS BORN thirty-four years ago, in New York, N.Y., so I have this fact in common with other mortals. After a thoroughly extrovert education, in New York and Pelham, N.Y. schools, I invaded the South for a three year stand at Washington & Lee University, Lexington, Va. The South won. Virginia is the second most beautiful State in the Union, the first being Connecticut where I now live with my wife and two children.

"As to the war, I tried to gain a Naval commission but my poor eyesight—without glasses turned me down. The local eye-doctor says I can't make the minimum 20-200 for the Army. I studied for my second class commercial radio-telephone and radio-telegraph licenses so that I may aid the U.S. Signal Corps in a civilian capacity. This hobby evolved from research I had to make on a short story. By the time I had finished the research I found myself a "ham" operator with my own station running 450 watts, now silenced for the duration, of course. Other hobbies, photography, medicine, model railroading, gardening, music, pistols, naval matters, *et al.*

"Since 1936 I've written five novels, the first of which *Not Too Narrow Not Too Deep* was subsequently filmed as *Strange Cargo* by MGM with Clark Gable in the leading role. I started on a series of brash and bizarre mystery novels for Simon & Schuster the first of which was *Lazarus*

No. 7, and latest *Passing Strange.* These coupled with the authorship of some 400 short stories and serials and my civilian defense work in the emergency radio communications network, keeps me pretty busy which is, of course, the only way to be.

www.ingramcontent.com/pod-product-compliance
Lightning Source LLC
LaVergne TN
LVHW091034080826
845145LV00002B/495

* 9 7 8 1 6 1 8 2 7 6 0 6 3 *